The Runaway IN LOVE

HELEN BRIGHT

VINCI
BOOKS

By Helen Bright

The Runaway Series

Vinci Books

vinci-books.com

Published by Vinci Books Ltd in 2025

1

A CIP catalogue record for this book is available from the British Library.
Paperback ISBN: 9781036707729

The EU GPSR authorised representative is Logos Europe, 9 rue Nicolas Poussion, 17000 La Rochelle, France
contact@logoseurope.eu

Chapter One

TESS

I'm not sure why I found Detective Constables Dickson and Twain—aka *Dickhead* and *Twatface*—so irritating today. Maybe it's because my period was due, and I was over-tired? Or maybe it was the fact that I'd been in this interview room for hours answering the same questions over and over. The same bloody questions I'd been answering for the past three days.

They both wore a smug smirk that they teamed with a regular eye roll. Until today, I'd kept my cool; the presence of Oliver Ward-Jones, my solicitor, being a calming influence. But now, with my period due and a severe lack of chocolate breaks, my anger had reached boiling point.

I knew Oliver could sense how wound up I was; he kept placing his hand on my arm whenever I raised my voice to the imbeciles. Honestly, I thought you had to be clever to join the police force, but it seems selective hearing was the only requirement when these two joined up.

Another officer had approached me yesterday morning while I waited for Dickhead and Twatface to arrive. PC

Foster was lovely. She listened to everything I had to say and didn't treat me like a criminal.

PC Foster had been in the police car that pulled up at The Willows before I ran away. I could have spoken to her that day, and maybe they'd have found Sarah sooner. But then the idiots in front of me now showed up, and I knew that telling them anything would have been pointless. Besides, from the information Kolya had gathered, Sarah was already dead. She'd been killed the day before, but for obvious reasons, I couldn't reveal I knew that.

When the detectives came to collect me for my interview/blame hurling, Kolya had spoken to PC Foster. At her suggestion, and with the advice of Oliver's colleague, he'd arranged a meeting with the chief inspector in charge of the force. He was going to make a formal complaint to sit alongside the one I'd made regarding the eye-rolling bastards in front of me.

As well as all the accusations of being involved in Sarah's disappearance and subsequent murder, I'd also been accused of prostitution. Not only pimping myself out to the men that Sarah and Beth had been involved with, but also to Kolya—my husband of only four days. Oliver raised all kinds of objections and insisted we take a break, but I'd heard it all before, and it didn't really bother me this time.

Kolya, however, was furious, and I'm sure the chief inspector will experience the full force of my husband's anger.

My husband… It seems so strange to say that. I have a husband—a handsome, mega-wealthy, powerful man who creates and sells weapons, has a son older than I am, and who can't leave his home without his bodyguards.

The man I took a bullet for.

The police wanted to know how I met my husband—

something else I couldn't reveal. We'd discussed at length exactly what I could and could not tell the police regarding my life after I left The Willows. Oliver suggested we say that Kolya spotted me standing in the doorway of his office building; he saw my clothes were wet from the rain and I was shivering. So, in an act of kindness, he offered to buy me new clothes and a hot meal. I told the detectives we clicked over dinner and fell in love right there and then. It was a lovely romantic story, and one I wished was true. But sadly, our first meeting was filled with chaos, bullets, and pain.

The police also accused me of being racist. Hassan had been spouting shit about me calling him a Paki—along with other girls whom he, Tariq and Farid had targeted. They told me they treated racism as a very serious matter. I laughed in their faces before replying, "It's a shame you didn't treat the sexual assault of a minor as a serious matter. My best friend would still be alive if you had."

The worst point in the interviews happened late yesterday afternoon when they revealed some truly horrific photographs.

I was heartbroken, angry, and physically sick when I saw what was left of my beautiful foster sister in that grassy marsh. I've seen police shows on TV where they reveal photos of long-dead victims, but nothing could have prepared me for the images of what remained of her decomposing corpse. Oliver called a halt to the interview, and I ran out of the room into Kolya's waiting arms, sobbing hysterically.

There was a commotion behind me, and when I turned around, Ivan had pinned Detective Dickhead against the wall and threatened bodily harm. Because of that, Ivan isn't allowed at the station anymore. The detective was going to press charges, but there was only his say-so regarding what happened. Neither Kolya, his guards, nor either of the solicitors had seen anything, *apparently*. And for some reason, none of the station's CCTV cameras had been working since I began my interviews.

I'd sat up all last night with the light on, being comforted by Kolya. Every time I closed my eyes, those images came back to haunt me. I wondered how long it would take for the memory of them to fade and be replaced by ones of a happier time.

"I asked you a question, Mrs Barinov, and I would appreciate an answer." Detective Twatface tapped his pencil against the writing pad he'd brought in to make him look professional or like he gave a shit.

I was about to ask Oliver to repeat the question when Dickhead added, "It's obvious you don't think this is important. You weren't even listening."

"Looks like you were contagious, then, fellas. After all, you've done nothing but ignore what I've said for days. I'd call at the pharmacy on your way home to see if they can give you anything for it. And while you're there, ask them if there's a cure for being complete and utter wankers. Personally, I think you're both too far gone for that kind of miracle. But you'll never know unless you ask." I finished with a wink and a smile, then stood.

"I suggest you sit down, Mrs Barinov. We're not done with you yet." Dickhead now had an extremely red face—one I was about to make a snide remark about until Oliver stopped me.

"Detectives, my client has been nothing but co-operative with both yourselves and PC Foster since the interviews began. However, due to the constant disrespect you have shown her, coupled with the accusations regarding her recent marriage, it's no wonder she's become so angry and upset. My client has suffered the devastating loss of her best friend—her foster sister—yet you've treated her worse than most criminals. Why? Throughout each of the interviews, I've tried to figure out why you've so much bitterness towards Mrs Barinov. The only time you've ever had dealings with her is when she's been the victim of a terrible crime. Do you treat all victims this way? I find it utterly deplorable. Therefore, I'll be making several complaints against both of you regarding the handling of these interviews, and make no mistake, I am not a man you can easily ignore. So I suggest you terminate this session forthwith. The time is now sixteen forty-four, in case you were wondering."

Twatface huffed and puffed before muttering, "Interview terminated at sixteen forty-four."

"We'll pick this up again tomorrow," Dickhead added.

"No, you won't," Oliver replied. "Mrs Barinov has a meeting with PC Foster at eleven o'clock, and as soon as that meeting has ended, she'll be leaving for her home in Oxford. If you've any further questions, I suggest you plan to visit with her there, and at *her* convenience."

As we turned to leave, Oliver placed his hand at the bottom of my back, ushering me out of the small, dull room.

Franco stood guard outside the door and took out his phone to call Kolya when he saw us.

The interview rooms were in a cool, windowless corridor, and as soon as we were let out into the main waiting room, the heat from the glaring sun as it shone through the windows hit us hard. Shading my eyes with my hand when the outer door opened meant I didn't see Kolya at first, but

5

I'd know those strong, comforting arms and the familiar manly scent anywhere.

"How are you, my darling?" His pale blue eyes took in my appearance while he hugged me close.

"I'm tired and cranky, Kolya, and I need chocolate and ice cream. Can we call somewhere on the way back to Jean's?"

"Of course, my love. Whatever you want. Though I must insist you ring Ivan as soon as possible. He's called every twenty minutes to see how you are."

"I bet he's driving Jean crazy," I mused.

"On the contrary. I believe she's had him doing a spot of DIY. He was up a ladder the last time we spoke."

We'd been staying with Jean at her house since we left Scotland. As there were seven of us in her three-bedroom, two-bathroom property, we had to get creative with the sleeping and bathroom arrangements. Kolya and I stayed in the room that Sarah and I used to share; Franco and Lucas shared the spare room; Ivan slept on the sofa bed in the living room, while Jonesy and Nate slept in the neighbour's caravan, which was parked on Jean's driveway. We could have gone to a hotel like Oliver and his associate, but I'd wanted to stay with Jean.

It felt good to be back again, but seeing our old room made me cry. I remembered all the fun times we'd had playing music and staying awake until the early hours— talking about insignificant stuff that seemed so important at the time.

Though we shared a room at The Willows, it was never the same there as it was when we'd lived with Jean.

Chapter Two

KOLYA

I was glad to be done with this poor excuse for a police station. On the first day of the interviews, my guards and I stayed all day in the waiting room. Although it appeared clean, there were strong scents of both urine and bleach, and there was chewing gum stuck to the undersides of the wooden bench seats. Names had been scratched into the honey-coloured pine, and there were drawings of male genitalia that varied in length and girth. I noted, from the artwork, that Dave woz ere 15/2/2012 and that Andy G was a grass.

The officer manning the front desk had asked us to leave the waiting area, and he ignored my request to speak to someone with higher authority. Oliver's associate, John Farrow, had suggested I request to speak with the chief inspector. He thought my financial status might influence the way we were treated and could keep us more involved in how the investigation was progressing. Considering my involvement in the death of Farid Ali, that wasn't a bad idea. Unfortunately, the chief inspector was on holiday and wasn't due back at the station until today, so we could do nothing but wait while they subjected my wife to hours of unnecessary questioning and harassment.

On our second day here, we were approached by an officer named Karen Foster, who also recommended I speak with the elusive chief. PC Foster pulled some strings and got us an appointment with him on his return this morning. The meeting proved less than helpful at first, with the man insisting both he and his officers had handled every aspect of Sarah's murder investigation by the book.

The solicitor beside me revealed page after page of ways in which the officers, and the force itself, could have handled things more efficiently. He also pointed to a lack of consideration and respect for both victims and witnesses. This information came from PC Foster in a meeting she'd had with Oliver and John at their hotel last night. It appeared that Karen Foster and several colleagues were frustrated with the way certain officers and upper management had handled the case. Of course, we couldn't reveal where the information came from, but there was enough in the paperwork that John spread out on Chief Inspector Carrick's desk to make him sit up and take notice.

When I told him I had enough contacts in both the media and UK government to take the information and complaints to a much higher level—Carrick's demeanour changed.

I've never played the *"do you know who I am"* card before. There are few in politics, the armed forces, and the financial sector who have not heard of KOLCAT, though hardly any know me personally. This man was most certainly not aware of me. So I left him with a parting gift: my name, company name, the names of both the UK Home Secretary and Secretary of State for Defence—who would be more than willing to speak on my behalf—and how much of my financial reserves I was willing to part with to enable the investigation to run more smoothly, and at a much faster pace.

John and I, along with my guards, waited once more on those uncomfortable bench seats before being approached by Chief Inspector Carrick around twenty minutes later. He shook my hand, then led us into a conference room before getting his assistant to serve us tea and coffee. Of course, I insisted we leave a guard in the waiting room to take care of Tess when she emerged from her latest round of questioning, although Carrick did better than that, letting Franco wait outside the interview room itself.

He informed me he was about to listen in to Tess's taped interview sessions so he could assess the way the detectives had handled them. It seemed either my status or wealth had an effect on the confidence he'd displayed earlier in his *"by the book"* team.

While waiting for Tess's questioning to end, I took a call I hadn't expected to receive after all these months. My technical security team had been doing what they do best, whether legal or not, to find out who my would-be assassin was. While they could find nothing about the shooter— which was odd as his face was captured quite clearly on CCTV—they'd identified the driver of the getaway vehicle, whose face was hidden by a baseball cap and sunglasses. Kevin had found a possible lead from a watch the driver wore that he'd singled out from just two frames of CCTV footage.

The driver had worn a custom-made Aebi watch. Kevin and Gustav—the man I relied on for international security and political advice—had finally discovered who the watch had been made for. It was probably given as a bonus for a well-executed hit.

Eitan Harel was ex-Mossad turned paid hitman. He was usually the man holding a gun, so why had he been the driver in my assassination attempt? If he'd been the one taking aim that day, I would have been a dead man, of that I am certain.

Originally from Sweden, Gustav Nilsson now lives in Berlin with his wife and young family, though he travels with me regularly when needed. He has contacts in many government organisations, so having him in my employ has proved invaluable. If anyone could set up a meeting with Eitan Harel, it would be Gustav.

I'd left the station to continue my conversation with Gustav in my car. My father always taught us that walls had ears, so when you're discussing something of a *sensitive nature*, it is best you do so in a safe place. My car is swept regularly for bugs despite the trust I have in my guards—another of life's lessons from my father.

After creating a plan of action with Gustav—who'd received the information Kevin had gathered—I stayed in the car to await my wife's return. The seats in the back of my bulletproof Mercedes S600 were much more comfortable than those in the conference room.

When I got the call from Franco informing me she was leaving, I hurried back inside the station to greet her. Yesterday she'd run out into the waiting area, sobbing heavily. When I found out what had caused her to cry, I wanted to put a bullet in both the detectives' skulls. She was so distressed she could not sleep and couldn't bear the light being turned off. Tess said that every time she closed her eyes, an image of Sarah's corpse would appear.

I held her in my arms all night and got her to talk about the fun times she and Sarah shared in the room where we'd been staying. There were photographs of both girls around the room and pin marks from where they'd put up posters of their favourite bands. I asked her to tell me about her happiest memory from the time she'd lived with Jean, and anything else I could think of to distract her from what she'd been going through at the station. Eventually, after the sun rose and the birds had trilled their morning song, we'd both fallen asleep.

Chapter Three

KOLYA

Tess wanted chocolate and ice cream, so we stopped off at a supermarket on our way back to Jean's house. I would have preferred to let one of my guards go into the store to purchase them, but my wife had insisted she wanted to go in herself. Lucas stayed outside while the rest of us followed Tess around with her shopping trolley, which she eventually let me push.

"It appears the trolley's broken," I told her while carefully trying to manoeuvre the wretched device around the aisles. I hadn't been in a supermarket since my years as a student, and I hadn't enjoyed the experience even then.

My guards at that time had found a great deal of humour watching Yannis, Chen, Imran, and I load our trolleys up with alcohol and microwavable meals. This time, Franco and Nate monitored security inside while Jonesy shopped from a list Ivan had texted him when he found out where we were heading. He and Jean had set up a barbecue in the back garden and wanted more steak and chicken. I overheard Jean insisting they'd bought enough earlier, but I knew my cousin would have eaten half of what they had by the time we arrived.

Jonesy threw in a few extra items he said we'd need, and then we added the sweet treats Tess had requested before making our way to the checkouts. Just as we got there, Tess said she'd forgotten something and darted off quickly to the left. Franco and Nate followed, despite her many protests. When they got back to the checkout, Tess seemed annoyed, and her cheeks were red. When I looked at what she'd placed on the conveyor belt, I knew why. A box of tampons and a pack of pads showed why she felt the need for chocolate and ice cream.

I glanced at each of my guards, noting all but Jonesy had their eyes elsewhere.

"From what you've just put on there and the amount of chocolate you're taking home, I'm surprised the detectives were still standing earlier. My auntie Annie's a lovely woman, but you could pit her against the devil himself whenever she was that way," he said, gesturing at the tampons.

Both Franco and Nate momentarily flicked their eyes towards Jonesy before resuming their security detail.

"I wanted to stab them in the eyes with the pens they hadn't used," Tess admitted. She breathed out slowly, then looked from Jonesy to me.

"Well, I'm glad you didn't. I'm not saying the mission to get you out of the cells when they locked you up for it wouldn't have been fun, but then we'd have had to burn the station down," Jonesy said. "PC Foster would have been out of a job, and she seems like a nice bird, as well as being fit as fuck."

"Jonesy," I warned, though I couldn't hide the smirk. I knew the policewoman had caught his eye. It was the swearing we were trying to curb around Tess; she needed little encouragement to use foul language. Jean said it was a way for Tess to let out her anger and frustrations with situations she couldn't control, and she'd certainly had enough of those in the last few months. But Tess will move in different circles now. We'd be dining with politicians and businessmen from around the globe in a little over two weeks, so she had to learn to control her need to use profanity.

I took hold of her hand and brought it to my mouth, kissing the back of it before doing the same to each of her fingers. I've no idea why I do that—I don't have a hand or finger fetish—but it's become something of a habit. Tess's hands are so slender and elegant. Even when she'd been sleeping rough on the streets of London, they looked like they belonged in a hand cream ad.

She leaned into me and sighed.

"Are you tired?" I asked before taking my wallet out and paying for the items that Jonesy was dutifully packing into carrier bags.

"I am. But I'm also hungry, and I need to shower away the smell and feel of the police station."

"I know what you mean. I want to wash away the day too. But tomorrow is our last visit, then we can go home."

"I'll miss Jean so much, though, Kolya. Staying with her has really helped. But I think it's been better having you and the guards there, too. Especially after yesterday," she said with a shudder.

"I would never have left you to deal with this on your own, Tess. You are my wife; it is my duty to be by your side whenever you need me."

Tess shook her head. "You'd have still been here even if

I wasn't your wife, and I want you to know how grateful I am, Kolya. For everything."

To my utter surprise, Tess grabbed the front of my shirt and pulled me down for a kiss. It was just a quick peck on the lips, but it meant more to me than anything because she had instigated it. It was the first kiss we'd shared since our wedding day, and I hoped it meant she was coming around to the idea that our marriage could be more than the arrangement she'd originally thought it would be.

Chapter Four

TESS

Why anyone would want to eat their steak rare was beyond me. In my mind, if it's still bloody or even slightly pink, it's undercooked. Yet every man here other than Lucas had it either rare or medium-rare. Even old Mr Hancock from next door ate it that way. He'd been chatting with the guards over the fence, telling them about his past military experience. He was enjoying their company and loved the fact that two of the guards were sleeping in his caravan. The old man thought he was doing his bit in some military-style operation by letting them use it. He knew what had happened to Sarah and had seen who the suspects were in the news.

Mr Hancock swore he wasn't racist by any means, then launched into a lengthy tirade about how there were more Muslims than ever in South Yorkshire and how the government shouldn't allow them to wear all their *"garb"* and build their mosques. "If they want to do that, they should bugger off back to where they came from," he declared.

Jonesy pointed out that most of the Muslims who

currently live in the UK were likely born here and should be allowed a place to worship the same as any Christian. He said he'd served in countries where people's right to worship, vote, and even attend school had been taken away, and he'd hate to live in a place where that could happen.

Mr Hancock went quiet when the rest of the guards agreed with Jonesy. Ever the peacekeeper, Jean steered the conversation around to DIY and complimented Mr Hancock on his new garden shed and water feature. He invited everyone around to have a look and tried to persuade them to try his home-brew wine and beer. Only Jonesy and Ivan had any alcohol. Franco went out to the caravan to keep a lookout over the front of the house with Dave—a guard I'd not met before. He and Lucas had stayed in the van while we'd been enjoying the barbecue in the back garden, though Nate had been delivering them food regularly.

By 9 p.m. I couldn't stop yawning, so Kolya suggested we go up to bed. He'd been watching me closely since we got back from the supermarket and had taken every opportunity to touch me, whether that was holding my hand or stroking up and down my arm while we waited for our food. The way he'd been looking at me was different too. His eyes seemed to take me captive—if that makes sense—and whenever I spoke to him or smiled, he made me feel like he owned my every word and expression.

Kolya gave me a look I'd never seen before, and I experienced several physical reactions. My mouth became dry, and my cheeks flushed. I gasped, feeling as though Kolya had removed all the oxygen from the air, and I had to look away so I could catch my breath.

He held my hand as we made our way upstairs, never once letting go until he closed the bedroom door behind us.

"Kolya, is there something wrong?" I asked. He shook his head as he closed the small gap between us, backing me up against the door.

"You kissed me today," he whispered, his breath hot as his lips ghosted against my ear. "I would like to reciprocate, if I may."

"Kolya..." I had no words, just his name and a gasp as he placed a hand behind my bottom and the other at the back of my neck.

"Shh, my love, I only want to kiss you. For now, anyway."

If he thought I didn't want it, he couldn't be more wrong.

Kolya pressed his lips against mine, delivering three chaste kisses before tilting his head, opening his mouth, and running his tongue against my plump bottom lip. I opened for him, flicking his tongue with my own, making him groan in my mouth while pressing even closer. His lips never left mine for even a second, devouring my mouth with a carnal hunger that had me grinding against him.

This wasn't just a kiss; it was making love with our mouths. It had me wanting things I'd only read about in my steamy romance novels. My nipples had grown to hardened peaks pressed against his solid chest, and I was so wet between my legs that it was almost embarrassing. Would this be the night I lost my virginity? Here, in Jean's house with all the guards around. The thought that someone would know what we were doing cooled my ardour, and I pulled away from our passionate kiss.

"Kolya, we can't do this! Not here in Jean's house with everyone around."

"Do what, my love? It was only a kiss." He smiled against my throat while placing lazy kisses up to my ear.

"You had me wanting so much more than kissing, Kolya, you know that. But I don't want our first time to be in a house full of people."

"Our first time? Did you think I was going to make love to you tonight?"

Kolya stepped away from me, running his fingers through his neatly trimmed beard and up to his hairline. I didn't know what to think. Wasn't that what he wanted? On our wedding day, he said he wanted more than just an arrangement. I'd felt his erection pressed against me, so I knew he was enjoying our kiss.

"I don't understand. I thought you wanted more. You said the vows we took meant something to you. Have you changed your mind again?" I felt so stupid. My inexperience had obviously given me the wrong impression.

I turned to leave, wanting time to myself to clear away the confusion in my head, but as I placed my hand on the door handle, Kolya stopped me.

Once again, he pressed me against the door, his chest to my back this time. His arms were on either side of my shoulders, caging me in.

"Do not run from me, Tess. Ever! And don't think that I don't want you—that couldn't be further from the truth. I want you *too* much. I have done for so long. But you're going through a terrible time right now, and you're not yet eighteen. I could not live with myself if I took advantage of you. When we come together for the first time, my love, it will have to be the right time for both of us. I love you, my darling, and I only want the very best for you, always."

"You love me?" I questioned, my voice quivering with emotion.

"I do. So very much," he replied, sighing as though a great weight had been lifted from his shoulders.

"I love you too, Kolya." I turned around to face him. "But just so you know, I'm more than willing to take things further."

He closed his eyes and took a deep breath in. "We can fool around a little, but I will not make love to you until you turn eighteen. I know it is the right thing to do, Tess, so I must refrain from taking it further until then. It will not be easy, my darling. After all, you are temptation itself. A beautiful goddess with flaming red hair and amber eyes that capture my very soul."

Chapter Five

KOLYA

Tess gave me a beaming smile and threw her arms around my neck. I bent slightly at the knee and picked her up, wrapping her legs around my waist before taking the few steps to her bed. I sat on top of the covers, pulling her core flush against my hard length.

"Take off your T-shirt," I whispered, then leaned back on my elbows, watching my teasing wife obey my order. She wore a white lacy bra that left little to the imagination.

Tess didn't speak or move, as if awaiting my next command. How far should I take this? Which sexual act might tip me over the edge? What touch, taste or sigh could force me to take my young wife's innocence?

In the end, it was Tess who made the first move, leaning forward to place her lips on mine. Our kiss was slow yet sensual, my desire for her increasing by the second. I abandoned her lips to trace my tongue from her neck to her lace-covered breasts, sucking on her tawny pink nipples through the delicate fabric. She gasped, then let out a breathy moan when I tugged on them gently with my teeth.

Tess rocked herself against my erection, the heat from her virgin sex blazing hot through the denim I wore. Grabbing her hips, I ground her against me, causing her soft moans and sighs to become more audible. A pink flush spread from her chest to her throat, and I followed it with my lips until they covered hers, swallowing her cries of pleasure when her orgasm hit.

As the last spasms of her climax ebbed away, she opened her eyes and gazed at me in wonder. At that moment, her beauty seemed almost ethereal.

She rested her forehead against mine and sighed contentedly.

"Was that your first orgasm?" I questioned. From her reaction, I knew the answer would be yes.

"You know it is. I'm a virgin, remember?"

"You don't need to have sex in order to come, Tess."

"Obviously," she said with a shy smile.

"How do you feel?" I asked.

"Good. Relaxed, but ready for more." She held her breath, awaiting my reaction.

"More?" I wasn't sure I could take any more tonight. Not without forgoing my good intentions and sinking my cock into her tight, wet heat.

"You didn't come. You could show me how to…get you off."

"Sex isn't a game where you take turns, Tess. Just because you came, it doesn't mean I have to."

"I know that, but I'd like to touch you, if that's okay. And I want to see you naked."

I groaned out loud at the thoughts and images her words created in my mind.

"I can't be naked, Tess. Not tonight. I'm tempted enough already."

22

"Just let me touch you, then. Show me what you like—how to hold you and make you come. Please, Kolya."

How could I deny my wife such a request? My cock was throbbing incessantly, straining against my zipper as if trying to escape into her waiting hands.

"Very well. Undo the button and lower the zip."

Tess ran the back of her fingers against my denim-covered length, causing my breath to hitch.

"Did that hurt?" she asked, pulling her hand away.

"God no," I groaned.

She moved her hand back to my crotch and swiftly opened my jeans. After parting the fabric, she gripped my cock through my boxers, tugging gently.

"Take it out," I commanded. I watched her pupils dilate before she went to do as I asked. It seemed my feisty young wife might be sexually submissive. Or was it just inexperience that made her react this way?

Just as she slipped her warm hand inside my boxers, there was a knock at the door, followed by Jonesy saying, "Boss, I think we have a problem."

Chapter Six

KOLYA

Tess moved off my lap and put on her T-shirt while I fastened my jeans. Her cheeks were red with embarrassment, and when I told Jonesy to enter, she turned away and faced the window.

"What's the problem, Jonesy?" I snapped, both angry and frustrated by the intrusion.

"Dave and Nate noticed a car registered to Hassan Akbar's father pass the house twice in the last ten minutes. They got a clear photographic image on the last pass."

"What? Did you get a look at the driver?"

"That's where we might have the problem, boss. We couldn't see the driver clearly, but the passenger looked like Hassan Akbar."

Tess gasped and turned to face Jonesy, her embarrassment now forgotten.

"It can't be him," she insisted. "Hassan was arrested. They locked him up."

She glanced my way with fear in her eyes. "Kolya, please tell me they haven't let him go."

24

I pulled her into my arms and held her tightly, kissing the top of her head before resting my chin there. I needed to call Oliver, but comforting my wife took precedence for the moment. Glancing over at Jonesy, I flicked my eyes to the side, indicating he should leave. Seeing Tess so fearful had upset him, I could tell, but until we knew if they'd released Hassan Akbar, I could offer neither of them any reassurance that everything would be well.

After ensuring Tess was okay, I told her to check where Jean was and to put the kettle on. I had a feeling this was going to be a long night.

After making several phone calls, an extremely irate Oliver informed us that Hassan Akbar was released without charge regarding Sarah's murder. However, there was a possibility he could face charges relating to various sexual offences, including the rape of an underage girl. Even with all that stacked against him, he'd been bailed for three weeks while their enquiries continued.

I could not believe the injustice, and neither could my guards. Franco in particular. He'd witnessed first-hand Farid Ali's recounting of Sarah's death, so he knew what Hassan was capable of. All my guards had read and listened to the signed confession, but to hear it in person made it seem even more chilling.

That Hassan Akbar was cruising the street so brazenly only highlighted how crazy this man was. No one could miss the cars parked outside and all six foot eight of Ivan as he stood in front of the door, arms folded, his glare menacing. Yet once again, they had driven up and down the street without a care, making it obvious they were watching the house when they slowed down as they passed.

Did they think that would intimidate us?

It had certainly done so with Tess and Jean, but that had soon turned to anger. They stood by the window, peeking through a gap in the curtains, each exclaiming how livid they were with the police for letting him go.

Leaving them to let out their fury, I went into the kitchen to discuss plans for keeping guard throughout the night. At present, he was just trying to scare us, but who knew if that would change?

While discussing our plan of action, I heard a loud smash, with further commotion outside the house. Ivan yelled Tess's name while she screamed to let her go. I ran towards the front door, followed closely by my guards. Tess was in Ivan's powerful grip, her back to his chest as she kicked and screamed, calling Hassan a murderer while swearing profusely. My guards surrounded us while Jonesy picked up Jean and carried her indoors. Hassan held his phone out of the car window, filming the whole thing, which meant retaliation wasn't possible. But when he made the shape of a gun with his free hand as if to shoot us, I saw red, and I tried to push my guards out of my way to get to him.

I wanted to take out Franco's gun and shoot the bastard between the eyes, but during our stay, my guards forwent their weapons so as not to frighten Jean. How I wish that were not the case.

My anger and frustration were so great I was shaking with ill-concealed rage. I demanded that Ivan take Tess inside, and although she protested both physically and vocally, he did as I asked. A grown man would find it hard to overpower my cousin; Tess didn't stand a chance. As soon as Ivan, flanked by Nate, took her inside the house, the car pulled away.

Before I could speak, Franco muttered under his breath, "Give me the order, boss. I'll take him out of the picture."

"No, Franco," I stated. "That job is all mine."

Chapter Seven

KOLYA

I waited with the rest of my guards outside Jean's property, watching until the car's headlights finally disappeared. Then I turned on my heel and stormed back into the house.

I was furious; my anger so strong it was almost palpable. How could the police have let him go after the evidence I supplied them with? How dare he threaten Tess? Why did she disobey my order to stay indoors?

She was arguing with Ivan and Nate when I entered the kitchen, screaming out her fury at being restrained. She looked wild and out of control; her hands shaking as she poked Ivan in the chest while yelling at him.

"Do not take your frustration out on Ivan," I bellowed. "He did the right thing when he restrained you and kept you safe. The man could have hurt you or taken you. Sarah is dead because of him, yet you put yourself in his path. Why, Tess? Why did you feel the need to disobey me and put yourself at risk?"

"Disobey you? Who the fuck do you think you are? You aren't *my* boss, and I've done without a father figure in my life for nearly eighteen years. I doubt I'd take notice of one now." Tess breathed fast and heavy; her eyes were wide, challenging me to argue.

"Do not yell and swear at me, Tess," I told her in a low, almost threatening tone. "I am your husband, and it is my duty to keep you safe. I will not hesitate to take the necessary steps to make that happen, whether you agree with them or not."

I did not wish to frighten her, but I needed Tess to know I meant business. No matter her anger, I'd lock her away from the outside world if I had to. I would rather suffer her wrath than see her hurt again.

"Are you trying to intimidate me, Kolya? That bastard out there tried to do it and didn't succeed. So, if I were you, I'd save your fucking breath and lecture someone you pay money to obey you. There's enough of them here. You could start with your cousin, he deserves it."

She turned swiftly, her copper curls flying behind her as she ran out of the room. I heard her footsteps come to a stop in the hallway when she came face-to-face with Jean.

"I'm sorry for smashing your plant pot, Jean. I was aiming for his head, but I missed it and hit the car bonnet instead. I'll buy you another when I can."

I heard a hitch in Tess's voice, as if she was about to cry.

"Don't worry about it, love. I never really liked that one, and the plant was dead anyway. Just make sure you take better aim next time, and use a bigger plant pot," Jean replied. Both of them laughed, which only increased my anger. But at least Tess wasn't crying.

Was Jean aware that Hassan was filming? Did she not realise he could go to the police with the evidence that Tess had tried to hurt him and had possibly damaged his car?

I didn't hear the rest of the conversation due to Dave

entering the property. He informed us the cameras he'd set up outside had captured the whole thing should we need it. I told him to send it to my email so I could show PC Foster when we went to the station tomorrow. She needed to know that Hassan was trying to intimidate Tess and Jean.

Even though Tess attacked his car, Hassan had taunted and provoked her by passing Jean's home so many times. He was the one who stopped and made a gun shape as if to shoot. From what Tess had told me, it seemed Hassan was fond of doing that. I, on the other hand, would make sure I held the real thing the next time I came face-to-face with Hassan Akbar. I can guarantee he won't be smiling when I'm done.

Jean came into the kitchen and went to put the kettle on, asking everyone if they wanted a hot drink. She took enough cups out of the cupboard and proceeded—with Jonesy's help—to make sure everyone had what they wanted. Jean thanked Jonesy, then brought me my tea.

"I'd like to have a word with you, if I may," she said as she sat down at the table. She gestured at the chair beside her, then glanced around the room at everyone present. "Would you mind leaving us, gentlemen? I won't keep him long."

Each of my men looked my way and only left the room when I nodded my approval.

"Do you have something on your mind?" I queried, keeping eye contact while taking a sip of my tea.

"I want to know why you married Tess. I know you have the resources to keep her hidden until she turns eighteen, which is only five weeks away. Why did you choose to marry her, Kolya? What was your aim?"

"Once the police found Sarah's body, they began questioning Tess's involvement. Was she also a victim whose body was yet to be found? Or did she play a part in her friend's death? The best chance Tess had was to come forward and give her side of the story. If I'd kept her hidden any longer, her absence would have made the situation much worse. Tess was a ward of the court, so she would have gone straight back into care if we hadn't been married. I couldn't have protected her like I'm trying to do now if she wasn't my wife."

I kept my eyes locked on hers, so she knew how important my next question was. "Now *you* can answer *me* a question, Jean. Why did you go outside with her instead of making her stay indoors? Why did you make out it was okay to throw the plant pot at him when he was clearly filming the whole thing?"

"Have you ever been so angry, hurt, and frustrated about a situation you throw caution to the wind and do something you know could backfire on you? Yet even knowing those risks, you still need to retaliate before you break down and succumb to despair?" she questioned.

I nodded slowly, still holding her gaze.

"You have a son, Kolya. If anything ever happened to him, God forbid, and the man responsible for it was outside your home, can you honestly tell me you wouldn't want to go out there and harm him somehow? Even knowing you could get hurt, you'd still do it, I'm sure. I'd say it's human nature to retaliate in that way.

"Because of my heart attack, Tess and Sarah were the last of my foster children. Maybe that's why the bond we had was so strong. They'd each lost their drug-addicted mothers in terrible circumstances, and there were no other capable family members waiting in the wings. So I became more than their foster mother, in a way. Despite being told they were only with me short-term, no one ever wants to adopt troubled teenagers. Good residential children's homes are scarce, so I knew they'd be with me until they were eighteen. That's what usually happened when I fostered teenagers who had no parents.

"I didn't have any kids of my own; my husband and I had problems conceiving. So I loved being a mother figure to all those who stayed with me, for however long I had them. I still see so many of them, even now. A lot of them have children of their own, and most are doing well." Jean took a drink of her tea, then sighed.

"What I'm trying to say is that I want that man to suffer. Not only was he involved somehow in Sarah's death, but he also tried to hurt Tess, and his actions tonight hurt her even more. The pain of Sarah's death has been like a knife to the gut for Tess and me, and what Hassan did earlier dug that knife in a little deeper.

"Tess isn't used to being told what to do. Growing up, she was always the one in charge, even at six years old. She'd looked after her mother and kept a roof over their heads for years, learning the hard way about budgeting and living off the state with an addict who thought of little other than her next fix. When she first came to live with me, it was hard for her not to take over and be the one in charge. It often resulted in her storming off upstairs in a temper, using swearwords that would make a sailor blush, but eventually, she came to trust me enough to let me take care of her wellbeing. The change in her once that happened was such a wonderful thing to see. She would laugh and act more like the teenager she was. Tess was always very protective of Sarah. They became as close as actual sisters, not foster sisters.

"Because of the situation tonight, I saw the angry, guarded Tess that first came to live with me. I saw how she bristled when you told her not to go outside. I knew she'd do it anyway, not just to defy you, but to let them know she wouldn't be bullied or intimidated. When I heard the door open and saw her dash outside, I ran out after her, thinking I could protect her somehow. But Ivan grabbed her as she threw the plant pot. It didn't hit its target, sadly, but it at least gave Tess the feeling that she'd gained back a little control. Like she'd shown them she was strong and could stand her ground. Tess didn't have that before. She feared he would hurt me if she told the police or retaliated in some other way, so she ran as far away as she could because she felt she had no other choice and no one to support her. After you had words with her in here, she probably felt alone and unsupported against Hassan once again, hence the shouting and swearing. So there was no way on earth I was going to tell Tess she was in the wrong, whether she was being filmed damaging his property or not."

I shook my head because she just wasn't getting it. "I will always support my wife, but I cannot have her putting herself in danger, Jean. The memory of her lying pale and bloody in my arms is still so fresh. I could not live through that again."

"I'm going to ask you once again, Kolya. Why did you marry Tess? And don't give me the excuse you did earlier, however plausible that is. I want the truth this time, from the heart."

After taking a deep breath, I admitted, "I married her because I'm in love with her. She's the first thing I think about on waking—which is only to be expected because she haunts my dreams every night. I know she's too young for me, and if I were a better man, I would have kept her safe and then set her free. But I'm not a good man, Jean. I allowed myself to become obsessed with her instead of just taking care of her as I promised. Once she turns eighteen, she will be my wife in *every* way, not just legally."

At first, Jean seemed confused, but then her eyes grew wide when my words finally dawned.

"What does Tess think about all of this?" she asked hesitantly.

"She understands more today than she did before. I should have told her sooner how I felt about her, but I didn't want to scare her away."

"And what about not consummating your marriage until she's eighteen? Who decided that?"

"I did. I'm not an ogre, Jean. And I do not prey on underage girls like the man we saw tonight. I respect Tess and her innocence, so I will wait. It is the right thing to do."

"For whom?" she questioned. "And just to clarify, when it comes to sex, Tess isn't underage. She's a young woman who knows her own mind and has been making decisions by herself for years. You're obviously a man who's used to being in charge, so you and Tess will clash if you try to take over her life. I know you spoil her, Kolya. You're an extremely wealthy man, so she'll have a comfortable life and will want for nothing. But a happy, lasting marriage needs more than that, especially when the people involved are so strong-willed. You keep calling her your wife, so act like a husband and make decisions together."

"Has Tess spoken to you about this?" I asked. I could tell that Jean was uncomfortable with our conversation, yet she seemed determined to see it through.

"We haven't gone into detail, but Tess was worried that you might be…disappointed. I wasn't aware you hadn't been intimate. I just assumed because you're married and you're sleeping in the same room…"

"I don't understand. Why would she think I'd be disappointed?"

"She doesn't have the experience you have, Kolya. You've been married before, and I'm sure you haven't been living like a monk for all these years. The only experience Tess has regarding sex was seeing and probably hearing all the men her mother earned her living from. I told her to talk to you about it and said it would get better with time. Like I've said before, I just assumed you were intimate. It's clear to see you're in love with each other. Your eyes never leave her when she enters a room. You have to be touching her—either stroking her hair or holding her hand. I've been a widow for some time, but I recognise the look of lust in your eyes when you gaze at her.

"My husband and I were very much in love. He was taken far too soon, but I consider myself a lucky woman to have had him as mine. We had the kind of love and…" Jean swallowed hard, then carried on speaking, "…desire for one another that most people can only dream of. I can see your relationship with Tess being like that. But you have to listen to her and not dismiss her feelings just because you think you know best. If you do that, she'll rebel; I guarantee it. You'll both have to learn to compromise."

"My priority is her safety, Jean. There will be no compromising on that."

She sighed heavily. "I'm not saying you should, but you're a clever man, Kolya, or so your business success dictates. You must realise that life will be a lot easier with a wife who feels happy, content, and respected, rather than an angry, screaming banshee."

I laughed a little, remembering the wild, out-of-control look of my furious young wife.

"Yes, Tess does have a quick temper," I stated.

"Oh, Kolya," Jean replied, shaking her head. "You don't know the half of it."

Chapter Eight

KOLYA

After getting Jean to agree to come back to Oxford with us, I had one last meeting with my security team, then sat in the back garden while I rang my son. The air was much fresher tonight, and I was glad of it. Sitting in the police station for the last few days had been stifling, and when everyone was together inside Jean's house, I felt confined. I longed for the space of my home in Oxford and the beautiful vista from the castle at Glengarran.

I didn't regret staying here, though. Tess wanted to be in her old home, and I know being with Jean helped. I admired the woman greatly. Fostering teenagers wasn't the easiest job in the world, especially ones with a troubled past. To me, she was an angel sent by God to tend to the failings of his human flock.

Since my mother passed away, I haven't bothered with religion, yet religious teachings have a way of staying with you. Though she lived all her life in Russia, my mother never favoured the Orthodox Church. She was brought up in a strict Catholic household and insisted all her children were baptised. My father, although distrusting of anyone with a higher power than himself, never denied my mother anything. So I went with her to church every Sunday until she was too sick to go. She always saw the good in people, even my father—the notorious pakhan. She would have adored Jean. The woman has an inherent goodness about her that makes you feel at ease, even when she's questioning you about your personal life.

Feeling a little calmer, I took out my phone and called my son, but James didn't answer. When the second call went to voicemail, I gave up. I could have contacted one of his security team, but I'd rather their focus be on him than on speaking to me. So instead, I dialled my best friend and prepared myself for yet another rant over my recent marriage.

Yannis answered on the fourth ring.

"What can I do for you, Kolya?"

"Good evening to you, too, Yannis. I've been calling my son, but he doesn't appear to be answering his phone. Are you with him?"

"We are out at Athena's. I've just stepped outside for a cigarette while he and Brad charm several young women with tales of their prowess on the football field, amongst other things. Do not worry; both his and my guards are in attendance."

Athena's was a nightclub on the island next to Athilos—the Greek island Yannis owns. It would be busy with tourists this time of year. I preferred it in the winter months when it was much quieter, and you could hear yourself speak. God, I sounded so old. I couldn't afford to be that way now that I had a young wife to entertain.

"Are you still angry with me?" I asked, though from his tone, I guessed the answer would be yes.

"Am I angry that I didn't get an invitation to your wedding? Me, your supposed best friend and godfather to your son? A little, I must admit. Yet I am more annoyed that you didn't tell me about your plans or that your feelings for the girl had changed. I could have talked you out of it, Kolya. I would have made you see sense."

"Don't start with this again, Yannis," I snapped. "I told you I had fallen for Tess. I wasn't prepared to live without her, so I had to make her mine."

"Because she saved your life? Kolya, you didn't have to tie yourself to her legally. Now she can take you for half of what you own, just because she happened to be in the right place at the right time. I'd say the little runaway had a tremendous stroke of luck the day she crossed your path."

Luck? Tess could have lost her life.

Images flashed unwelcome in my mind. Memories of her pain-filled cries and blood-soaked clothes as we transported her to the hospital.

"I can't believe you just said that, Yannis."

My voice was low, my tone cold. I would tolerate no one speaking so flippantly about the day Tess was shot. He was there; he saw the whole thing. How could he be so callous?

Yannis took a deep breath and held it—as if he was about to say something but thought better of it.

"I'll get in touch with James tomorrow," I informed him.

Before I could hang up the call, Yannis cleared his throat and, in a quiet voice, declared, *"I'm sorry, Kolya. I shouldn't have spoken about your wife in such a way. It was disrespectful and totally uncalled for. I hope you can forgive me."*

I didn't answer straight away. Despite his apology, I was still so angry at his words, especially after what had happened here this evening.

"Kolya, you've been my best friend for over twenty years. I don't want to see you go through what I have in a marriage. My first wife fucked my father; my last two fucked me financially. I would hate to see you go through the same thing."

"We've been over this already, Yannis. And you've spoken to Tess several times in our video chats. Surely you can see she isn't a gold digger. She doesn't covet status or a lavish lifestyle like your ex-wives."

"They can change, Kolya. I've seen it happen. I can't believe you couldn't enforce a prenup."

"That wasn't an option, my friend, and even if it was, it wouldn't have been necessary."

"But what about James? How will he fare financially if she takes you for half of what you have? And what about me? As James's godparent, you put me in charge of his finances until he turns twenty-one, should anything happen to you. Will the agreement still stand now he has a stepmother? One who's two years younger than him, with no idea how to manage a billion-dollar company, I might add."

"Oliver has arrangements in place to secure James's future, and that of KOLCAT, but as my wife, Tess will be well taken care of when I am no longer around."

"So, am I to take it you no longer wish me to be his financial guardian?" Yannis let out a sigh as he said this, as if disappointed.

When Catherine passed away, I rewrote my will, giving Yannis legal guardianship over James in the event of my death. It included managing my son's substantial inheritance, which he'll receive on his twenty-first birthday.

"Oliver said that wouldn't be an issue, and I hope James can still come to you for any advice if he needs to," I added.

"Of course he can. James can come to me for anything, you know that. And he knows it, too. But I was also wondering what I should do about my will. As you know, James will inherit everything I own—

including Athilos—with you overseeing the entire process until he comes of age. I need to know that if anything happened to both of us, your wife couldn't challenge those documents. After all, you stand to inherit everything should the unthinkable happen to our boy."

"God, Yannis, don't go there tonight. I've had too much to deal with already. And in any case, our lawyers ensured there could be no legal challenges to either of our wills as far as my son's inheritance is concerned. I needed to do so to prevent my father from becoming James's legal guardian and taking over KOLCAT. I don't want my son involved with the Bratva, never mind my father getting his hands on my business. Every government outside of Moscow would have a fucking fit if that happened."

Yannis laughed loudly before giving an order, likely to one of his guards, to bring him another drink.

"Yannis, are you drunk?" I questioned.

"Not nearly enough, my friend, but I'm hoping the next one hits the mark. You're not the only one who's had things to deal with today," he replied with a touch of frustration.

"Ahh, your cousins are still trying to exercise their right to vote. I have to say, Yannis, as shareholders, they are entitled to voice their opinions."

"They veto everything I propose, though, Kolya, no matter how beneficial it would be. We need to branch out into other avenues. There's no money to be made in the ship-building industry anymore. The Americans are running the cruise ship market, and the Arabs have seen more growth in their luxury liners and hotels this year than we have in the last five. If it wasn't for my father investing so much in oil, we might face difficulties."

"How about the other shareholders? Do they have much to say?"

"The ones who worked with my father are like sheep, following the ways of the old shepherd. They make it difficult when I try to guide

41

them to more bountiful pastures. Before the recession, it didn't matter. No effort was needed to pull in new business. They came to us. Then, boom, the big financial fuckup paved the way for the thieves from the Middle East. They took over the hotel and leisure industry one fucking gold brick at a time."

"You need to take a break, Yannis. Come to Oxford and stay with us for a while. You can officially meet Tess and put your fears about her to rest," I told him.

"I will, as soon as I present the revised proposal before the board. I have meetings in London and Paris next month, so I will visit you and your new wife when they have ended."

"I look forward to it, Yannis. Now go inside and keep an eye on my son. The older he gets, the more I worry."

_____

After bidding Yannis goodnight, I went upstairs to the room I shared with Tess. The light was off, and she was feigning sleep. I knew she was still awake and silently seething when I slid into bed beside her and her elbow made contact with my ribs.

"Ow, Tess, what the hell was that for?"

"Fuck off, Kolya. You aren't stupid. You know why I'm mad at you," she hissed.

"How did you expect me to react? You put yourself in danger by going outside."

"He was sitting in a car, Kolya, and I knew Ivan and Dave were out there too."

"He could have had a weapon. You could have been lying in a pool of blood once again. Did you think about that? Did you, at any time, stop and think how the people who love you would feel if that happened? Or do you just not care about any of us?"

"Of course I care. I just wanted to wipe that horrible fucking smile off his face, and possibly bash his skull in with something hard and heavy. I spotted the plant pot and thought that would do."

"I know you are angry and frustrated, Tess, but you must be sensible about this. Hassan was filming you. He could go to the police with the threats you made and the damage you did to the car."

"But he drove here, Kolya," she whined. "Surely the police will see that's intimidation."

"They might give him a warning, but at the end of the day, neither you nor Jean have a restraining order against him, and as long as the driver pays his car tax, he is entitled to drive on any public road."

Turning to face me, she said, "I can't promise I won't do it again, Kolya. I want to see the same injuries on him as Sarah had in those photos. I wish he were rotting in a boggy marsh somewhere like she was."

A thin sliver of street lighting shone through a gap in the curtains, highlighting her pale features and determined expression. Sliding my arms around her shoulders, I could feel how tense she was. We needed to sleep, yet she was so wound up with anger and frustration I knew that wouldn't happen anytime soon. Unless...

"Tess, you know I would do anything for you, don't you?"

"So you say," she replied dismissively.

"Well, know this, my darling. You will get your wish, but you must do something for me in return. If we encounter Hassan again before we leave, keep your cool. You must remain calm and aloof and act like he's not even there, and above all else, you need to let me keep you safe. Do you understand what I'm saying, Tess?"

"Yes, I think so," she said hesitantly. "What are you—"

"Shh," I whispered. "You do not need to speak of it or worry about it ever again. Just be content that the amount of time Hassan Akbar has left is extremely limited."

Tess nodded her head before snuggling into me. I held her tighter, glad that my words had not caused her to fear me. Even though our bodies were pressed together so tightly in a narrow single bed, there was nothing sexual about it. How could there be, when Tess lay there knowing that her husband was going to kill for her? Again.

Chapter Nine

Jean was busy packing her case ready for our trip to Oxford, so Jonesy offered to cook breakfast. Jean had insisted on serving the men a hearty full English breakfast every morning since our arrival. I think she's enjoyed cooking for everyone. Although she tries to keep herself busy with various activities, she said she'd felt quite lonely since she had to give up fostering. I could understand that. I felt bad that I wouldn't be living in the same town anymore, but Kolya said Jean could stay with us whenever she wanted.

He'd been so sweet this morning, kissing me awake and bringing me tea and toast in bed.

I'd got my period through the night, and although I'd bought pads and tampons in the supermarket yesterday, I'd been in such an angry mood when I came to bed, I'd forgotten to put on a pad just in case. As per usual, I'd leaked through my pyjama bottoms, so there was blood on the sheet. I was mortified, but Kolya took it in his stride. Despite my objections, he stripped the bed, then took the sheet into the bathroom to rinse with cold water. He demanded my pyjamas too, but I wouldn't let him wash those. I was embarrassed enough already.

I asked him how he knew it was best to use cold water to remove blood stains, forgetting he was married before, then hating myself for being jealous of a dead woman. Kolya said Nan had taught all the men about soaking bloodstained fabrics in water. She was fed up with the towels in the gym getting stained when the men had got a little too rough in the ring. Nan hated using strong chemical stain removers and favoured a more natural approach wherever possible. So she'd laid down the law and insisted they soak everything in the buckets she provided, telling them if she found anything lying around that hadn't been pre-soaked, she would bin it.

I missed Nan. I'd become so close to her over the last few months, which was understandable, as I'd seen her almost every day. She'd called me every night since I'd been here, and I'd cried down the phone to her the day they'd shown me those photographs of Sarah's body.

I couldn't wait for Jean to meet Nan. I'm sure they'll become friends. They're nearly the same age and are alike in so many ways.

I'd apologised to Ivan and Nate this morning. All that screaming and swearing at them last night was uncalled for, and I worried that I'd hurt Ivan while I was thrashing around when he'd restrained me. Not that I could move much. The man is a six-foot-eight wall of muscle.

Neither Nate nor Ivan seemed bothered or upset by my behaviour towards them last night. They were more concerned about my feelings over the situation.

Ivan didn't want me to go to the station to see PC Foster and asked if we could get her to come here instead. I just wanted this last visit out of the way so we could all go home.

Home. To actually have a place to call home is a dream come true, but the fact that my home is a huge sprawling estate with two swimming pools, a basketball court, a home gym, and a shooting range is truly something else. Add in the Scottish castle and the hotel in London, and I feel like I should have HRH beside my name.

Jonesy turned up the radio and belted out the words to a song I recognised from Jean's *Hits of the '60s* album. The song was "Young Girl" by Gary Puckett and the Union Gap. I knew the song was about a man finding out the girl he's seeing is underage, but when Jonesy started singing it—first to me, then to Jean—the expression on Kolya's face changed from amused to brooding. As if he was worried about something. I went over and hugged him, but he didn't hug me back. He just smiled a sad smile and told me it was time to go.

I didn't like the room that PC Foster had escorted us to. It wasn't like the opposing, grey-walled interview room where I'd been questioned all week. In fact, it was quite the opposite.

It had ivory-coloured walls with pretty paintings of spring flowers and bluebells in woodland—a sight I normally love to see. The seating couldn't be more different to the heavily scratched plastic seats in the interview room, either. There were three comfortable high-backed leather-look chairs and a matching two-seat sofa. An oak-effect coffee table stood between them. Oliver had moved one of the chairs around so he could sit beside Kolya while PC Foster and her colleague, PC Winters, *chatted* with us. The room was designed to put people at ease, but all I could think about was how many victims of rape and other forms of abuse and assault had sat on this same sofa and looked at the same paintings, their eyes filled with tears as they recounted the terrifying moments that brought them here.

Kolya had shown the officers the video of Hassan that Dave had recorded last night. I hadn't looked at it. I didn't want to get angry again—not in front of the police, anyway. You couldn't fail to hear all the shouting and swearing I was hurling Hassan's way. To be honest, I felt a little embarrassed. I hadn't realised it had sounded so bad. No wonder Kolya tells me off when I do it.

I shook my head and closed my eyes, making a mental note to try taking a step back and counting to ten the next time I was in a situation where my anger was getting the better of me. Whether it would work or not, I wasn't sure, but I was willing to try, for Kolya's sake.

Listening to PC Foster talk about Lisa and Ben, the residential social workers who worked at The Willows, was the first test of whether I could control my angry outbursts. She was explaining the steps that Lisa and Ben had taken to try to manage Sarah's rebellious streak. I laughed when she told me how worried they'd been when Sarah and I disappeared.

"Don't make me laugh," I told her. "Lisa didn't give a shit about me and Sarah. She was against us right from the start."

"What makes you say that?" asked PC Winters.

"She wouldn't take us to visit Jean at the hospital. Then, when Jean was better, Lisa stopped her coming to see us at The Willows."

"From the notes I have regarding the exact situations you've just mentioned, it appears that Lisa had very good reasons to deny both. I can't let you look at the records we were given when you and Sarah went missing, but I can tell you that Lisa made enquiries about taking you and Sarah up to the hospital. Your caseworker got together with the rest of her team and decided that seeing Jean so poorly would be too traumatic for both Sarah and you to handle. Stopping Jean from going to visit you and Sarah at The Willows after her recovery was because of Sarah's behaviour every time Jean left. From what I read, Sarah would become tearful, which would then lead to destructive and violent behaviour once the tears subsided. Do you recall Sarah acting this way, Tess?"

"Well, yes. But it wasn't that bad. Not really."

"So threatening to smash all the windows and set fire to the building if they didn't let her go back and live with Jean wasn't that bad? Or perhaps you think getting into fights with other children and throwing things at the staff was acceptable behaviour? Tell me, Tess. What else could Lisa have done in that situation? She had other children to think about and protect, too, not just you and Sarah."

"They could have done more to stop her meeting Farid, Tariq, and Hassan," I insisted. "But they were no help at all."

"I have seen several pages of notes regarding Sarah's ongoing disappearing acts. How she kept cutting the wires to the alarms on the windows as soon as they'd been fixed; how Ben had noticed her leaving one evening and followed her to where a car was waiting. The car drove away before he could memorise the plates. Sarah screamed and spat at him when he tried to take her back into the property. She blamed him for them leaving and didn't speak more than two words to him after that. And they weren't ones you would repeat in polite company.

"When you reported Sarah to the teacher, her caseworker was already trying to find a place for her in another residential children's home or foster. But there aren't many foster families around who would have the ability to cope with teenagers with such…challenging behaviour, and those that could help were already full. During those few days she spent in the other home, she exhibited no behavioural issues whatsoever."

I placed my hands over my eyes. Having her mention things that Sarah had got up to brought memories of those turbulent times back to the forefront of my mind. Yes, at times, Sarah could be difficult, but it wasn't often. Hearing PC Foster talk about those incidents felt wrong. She was no longer here to defend herself. Sarah came into foster care having previously lived in a similar situation to me, but hers was much worse. Her mother and stepfather had been abusive and thought nothing of beating Sarah, even as a toddler. They'd passed away in a drunk driving accident when Sarah was eleven, giving her a welcome reprieve from their constant abuse.

No wonder she often became violent. Until she went to live with Jean, she'd known little else.

I felt like I had to tell them about the real Sarah. The one I loved like a sister. So I told them all about how she used to help the younger kids with their maths homework. Sarah was brilliant at all kinds of mathematics. She just got stuff like that. Not like me. I was rubbish at it. I also told them how she'd stick up for those weaker than her. She hated bullies and would always try to protect those who were scared and vulnerable. She just didn't know how to take care of and protect herself. That was my job, and I'd failed epically.

I couldn't stop the tears from falling once again. If only I had done more to help her. I should have reported Tariq and the rest when she first went to meet with them. Yes, she might have been moved, but at least she'd still be alive.

Kolya put his arms around me and held me tightly. I knew Oliver was speaking to PC Winters, but I couldn't quite hear what they were talking about due to my sobbing. The only words I did catch were from PC Foster, who wanted to wait until I'd calmed down enough to carry on.

I shook my head and insisted we get this over with as soon as possible. I wanted to be where I felt safe, and it wasn't anywhere near Fellbrook Police Station.

"Tess, I'm not defending anyone. I just want you to let go of some of your animosity towards the staff at The Willows and concentrate on everything else that was happening in the weeks leading up to Sarah's disappearance. I want to know everything she told you about the men she was meeting with. Did she mention what type of cars they drove? Where they'd take her? If she knew where they lived? I need you to give me a full description of each of these men. What colour hair did they have? How did they style it? Did they wear jewellery or have tattoos? You need to tell me everything she did with them, willingly or not.

"I know it's going over everything again, but I need to hear it from you when you're not being defensive like you were with Detective Constables Dickson and Twain. I want to know everything, even if you think it's not that important to the case. Let *us* decide what we can use to help catch those who hurt Sarah. Start from the very beginning and leave nothing out. Use your own words, as if you were speaking with a friend. I know your life has changed a lot over the last few months, and you're married now. But forget about that and be who you were back then. Tell me your hopes and fears for Sarah during that time. And I want to know everything about the day you ran away. What made you make that decision?"

"I've already told your colleagues all this. And anyway, there are photos of all the men on Sarah's phone. You could just get them from there," I told her, my voice raised in frustration.

"We don't have Sarah's phone, Tess. She didn't have any possessions with her when she was found," PC Winters stated before glancing at PC Foster.

"Do you happen to know Sarah's mobile number?" PC Foster asked. Her pen was poised on the paper waiting for my reply. Kolya squeezed my hand in reassurance, but when I looked at him, he gave the slightest shake of his head, his ice-blue eyes narrowing ever so slightly. I was confused. I thought the police had Sarah's phone. Or, at least, her SIM card, along with the signed confession from Farid Ali.

I turned back to PC Foster and told her no, I never had a phone at The Willows, so there was no need for me to have her number. But Beth had it. I also told her about the fight Beth and I had the day I ran away. I then proceeded to tell her everything she'd requested, right from the time we first met Tariq when he worked at the local youth club. Both she and PC Winters listened attentively, rarely stopping and interrupting as Dickhead and Twatface had done. What's more, their expressions remained neutral or, when warranted, understanding. They didn't express any scorn or judgement or disbelief.

Two and a half hours after we first entered the station, we finally got up to leave. PC Foster informed us they would be in touch as soon as they had any leads. They gave me a number to call in case I remembered anything else and promised they'd do everything in their power to see that those responsible for Sarah's death would be brought before the courts.

Both Kolya and I thanked them, along with Oliver, and I swear I saw tears in PC Foster's eyes when she said she was happy to see me safe and well after being missing for so long.

When we stepped out of the station into the bright sunlight, I felt as though a heavy weight had been lifted from my shoulders, yet I also felt drained. Trying to remember what details I had to keep hidden from the police was so tiring. Several times, I had to stop and take a deep breath before I revealed anything that could incriminate Kolya. He helped with that, of course. If I was about to say something that could lead to further questioning, he would bring my hand to his lips and kiss my fingers or gently massage the nape of my neck. A loving gesture from husband to wife in a distressing moment was all the officers saw. Not the warning it really was.

Chapter Ten

KOLYA

Within an hour of us landing at our home in Oxford, I was back in the air and on my way to London. I had business in the capital, but that wasn't until tomorrow. I could have stayed the night with my wife, but after this morning, touching my young bride felt wrong. Though I still desired her desperately.

When she'd stood there this morning blushing with embarrassment, trying to hide the fact that she had bled through her nightwear onto the sheets, I saw even more clearly how young and vulnerable she looked. Her teddy bear pyjamas only added to her teenage appearance. But her actions... The way she'd wrung her hands together with her eyes downcast, unable to meet my gaze; her embarrassment growing when I'd offered to soak the bloodstained clothing. The fact that she was so ill at ease with something so natural made me stop and consider how she would feel when I finally took her virginity. Would she be as upset if she bled then? When the evidence of our lovemaking left her body, would it embarrass her so much that she would hang her head in shame?

If this morning had taught me anything, it was that Tess wasn't ready for a sexual relationship—something I had known all along. Our time at the police station reinforced this knowledge. The way she became so defensive when PC Foster told her the truth about the social workers in charge at The Willows. It was obviously something she hadn't wanted to hear, and she'd reacted in much the same way as James used to whenever I'd pointed out that he was wrong.

Yet knowing all this—seeing with my own eyes why my relationship with Tess was so wrong—I still wanted her. My hunger for her had not waned; my love for her increasing with each passing day. What kind of monster did that make me?

I had never desired younger women the way some of my business associates have. I know several middle-aged men who seem to think having a young woman on their arm, or in their bed, shows they still have the same virility they had in their youth. They use those women as a physical statement, as if to show they have what it takes to stay on top in our competitive, egotistical business arena. An additional weapon to keep them in the game, if you will.

When you deal in arms, you deal in power, and nothing makes a man feel more powerful than bringing a woman to orgasm. Often, men seem to think that proving their sexual prowess and stamina with a woman much younger than themselves makes them some sort of champion. I have never understood that mindset. Age is just a number—for both men and women. It should have no bearing on how much pleasure you feel when you take the time to know your lover's body and identify what they need to take them over the edge. Helping a woman achieve an intensely satisfying climax is a challenge all men should rise to. But keeping the woman you commit your life to happy and sexually satisfied for the rest of your days… that's where only those worthy of her commitment succeed.

My father says you can judge a man's loyalty by the way he treats his wife. If he isn't faithful and his wife is unhappy, you can do business with him, but you should never trust him. If he finds it so easy to betray the woman who takes his name and bears his children, he will have no qualms about betraying you. For all the terrible crimes my father and his organisation have committed over the years, in this, I feel, he knows what he's talking about.

I saw first-hand the devastation that infidelity in a marriage can bring. Yannis was a wreck when his wife left him for his father. They'd been having an affair for months, and the betrayal broke something inside my friend. He was a changed man after that, even with those close to him, including me. James was the only one to make him smile. He brought him out of the depressive, angry, vengeful state he'd been in since he'd discovered their affair. Although, after the explosion on his father's yacht, he withdrew once again for a while.

"Boss, Omari just called to let us know that Prince Amir will arrive with eight guards at one thirty tomorrow afternoon. Two of the guards will stay in the lobby as per protocol, while the rest will accompany the prince to your suite. Greta has arranged the usual regarding food and drinks," Jonesy confirmed.

"Are we still heading to Berlin tomorrow night?" he asked.

"Yes. I'd like to be in the air as soon as the prince leaves. I don't expect our meeting to last longer than three hours, so I thought we could request a flight time of around six thirty. We'll need to take the helicopter instead of driving, though. The last time we attempted to get to Heathrow by road during rush hour was a disaster."

"Don't remind me," Jonesy said with a groan. "The only thing worse than driving through London in rush hour traffic is driving through New York during rush hour traffic. I don't know how taxi drivers deal with the stress."

I nodded my agreement. Before I could comment, my phone screen lit with an incoming call.

"Gustav, how are you? Please tell me you've set up a meeting with Harel."

"Kolya, he's unreachable. My Israeli contact confirmed Mossad will block any attempt to reveal Eitan Harel's whereabouts but assured me he no longer poses any threat to your safety." Gustav sighed, then added, *"I can understand the need to speak with him regarding the attempt on your life, but I feel it is my duty as your friend, as well as advisor on these matters, to tell you to think very carefully about how you respond."*

"I assume you told them we only want to find out who hired him, not to bring him harm?" I queried.

"Of course, but you knew he wouldn't give up that information, Kolya."

"There are many ways to gain information, Gustav," I replied. My mind had conjured up several scenarios in which I could make the men involved in the shooting suffer.

"Kolya, I can understand your anger. But going up against Mossad would be suicide."

"Gustav, letting my attempted assassination go unchecked is suicide. Fuck Mossad. If the Israelis want to dig their heels in over this, then so will I. Any bids they have for weaponry are off the table until I meet with Eitan Harel. That includes the deal I was about to agree on regarding the defensive radar missile system."

Gustav made a whistling sound. *"The Americans won't be happy about that."*

"That's what I'm counting on," I informed him.

"I'll let them know," he replied. *"I wonder how long it will take Caroline Dawson to get in touch."*

"Make her aware I won't appreciate being contacted directly about this. Let her stew awhile. I'm sure she already knows about my meeting with the Saudis tomorrow, but it won't hurt to mention it either way. If she thinks there's another major player interested in making a deal for the system, that might be the incentive she needs to plead our cause."

Caroline Dawson—the ex-CIA security operative, now a European-based US Defence Attaché—will do her best to keep the deal on the table while defending the Israeli stance on this. She thinks we have a good working relationship because I treat her position with the respect it deserves, yet I know plenty who don't. Internationally, weaponry and defence have always been male-dominated businesses, and many would like to keep it that way. They think women are too *soft*, too caring, and always supporting the underdog. They could not be more wrong in Caroline Dawson's case, which is probably why the US government gave her that role. It could have been created just for her.

No one who's ever had dealings with Caroline Dawson would say she was soft. She's an aggressively intelligent woman who spent many years working her way up through the CIA into central government. She's a woman who prides herself on getting the job done and makes it her business to know who's who in the world of weaponry and defence. Caroline comes across as friendly and *on your side*. But make no mistake, she is all about her country and its political agendas. Once CIA, always CIA. It's in her blood.

I made the mistake of having sex with her. Twice. Not my best decision, either time. But she's an attractive, powerful woman who knows how to turn on the charm, and during the first couple of European functions she attended in her new government position, we ended up back at her hotel. Caroline prefers to be sexually dominant, which doesn't really work for me. I should have said no the second time she invited me back; I knew that. But loneliness can often lead us to make choices we later regret. Caroline seems to think that because we fucked, she has some sway over me.

She could not be more wrong.

I am a man who listens to advice given by those I respect, but ultimately, any decision I make regarding any aspect of my life is my own. It has to be for someone in my position.

"Have you decided which guards will accompany you if the Israelis give in to your demands?" Gustav asked. I could hear the faint clicks of a keypad. No doubt he was already putting a logistical plan in motion.

"Jonesy, Nate, Lucas, Rashid, and Donovan," I informed him.

"I'll get things in motion on my end. Email me your flight time and any other details regarding your stay. You'll have a driver waiting when you land, and there'll be a backup vehicle as per the usual protocol. I assume you'll be staying at the hotel?" he queried.

"Yes, though I would be thrilled if you and your beautiful wife would join me for dinner. How is Erika?"

"She is well, but extremely tired. Erika doesn't seem to be managing this pregnancy as well as the last three. She's been quite anaemic and has suffered many headaches."

"No wonder she is tired, Gustav. She manages her own

company, has three children under ten, and is due to give birth to another in a couple of months."

"I know. That's why I have arranged for Mari, our part-time nanny, to work more hours. Erika wasn't happy about it at first, but she likes and trusts the woman, and they have become great friends over the years. I know there will be no more babies for us after this one is born. How about you, Kolya? Do you plan on having more children now that you are married?"

"It is early days for us, Gustav. Tess will probably want to live a little before she becomes a mother."

I hadn't really thought about another child until my father mentioned it. James is his only grandchild. My brother Aleksei and his wife had problems conceiving, and after many failed attempts at IVF, they gave up. My eldest brother has never been married, much to my father's annoyance.

"Are you planning on having a honeymoon? I know you mentioned the issues Tess has been having with the police, and now this business with Eitan Harel, but I thought you would want to whisk your wife away to the Caribbean and spend some quality time with her. It can't be easy being apart from each other so soon after your marriage."

Gustav was right. It would not be easy being apart from Tess. It hasn't been since the day we met. But then, neither was it easy to be around her without making love to her. I am damned either way.

"We will make time soon. Perhaps we will combine Tess's birthday celebrations with an extended honeymoon. Her birthday is just a month away; we don't have long to wait."

Just over a month before I claim my wife in the most intimate way possible. Five weeks of longing that will only increase with each passing day. To be near her would be torture. My idea of spending as little time as possible with her was the right decision. It didn't mean I couldn't speak to her or see her. Technology will cover that.

"Kolya, I have to go; I need to get in touch with my Israeli contact. I will let you know their response as soon as I receive it."

"Thank you, Gustav. Give my regards to Erika and say hello to the children for me."

"I will. See you tomorrow evening at the hotel, Kolya. And don't be surprised if Caroline Dawson finds you."

Chapter Eleven

KOLYA

The hotel in Berlin had undergone a substantial refurbishment in the last six months, though we'd kept the period features Catherine's father had adored. He bought the hotel a month before the fall of the Berlin Wall and restored many of its original architectural features, bringing it back to its former glory. James Lassiter was a man who had the foresight to know what would appeal to future discerning travellers.

Flanked by my security team, I walked through the foyer towards the private elevator that would take me up to the penthouse suite. I kept the penthouse suite for myself in each of the hotels. It meant I could keep the rooms secure, and my team could regularly sweep for bugs and other tracing equipment. It gave me peace of mind during my travels and also reassured my various business contacts. They knew that anything we spoke about would not be heard elsewhere.

Just before we reached the elevator, a familiar blonde who wore a friendly yet determined look approached us.

"Kolya, I need to speak with you immediately. People aren't happy with the threats you made regarding a recent deal."

"Miss Dawson, what a pleasant surprise," I replied, forcing a smile, though I did not break my stride.

"Cut the crap, Kolya. You knew I'd be here, just like you know you can't pull out of the d—"

"Caroline, you should know that I don't respond well to being told what I can or cannot do. Despite how well negotiations were going, I have to make a decision I am happy with, and at present, I find I am not happy with the bid I received nor the people who offered it."

As I stepped into the elevator, Caroline demanded that we sit down and discuss the situation. She tried to follow but was stopped by Jonesy, who warned her she should take a step back. Before the elevator doors closed, Caroline requested that we meet to discuss my *"unreasonable behaviour."*

"Have a pleasant evening," was all I said as the doors finally closed.

"She didn't look happy," Jonesy commented with a hint of laughter in his voice.

"I agree. It will be interesting to find out how long it will take her to set up the meeting with Eitan Harel. I assume Gustav will be inundated with calls and requests from her over the next few hours. It will make for interesting conversation over dinner this evening," I told him.

"Are you dining in the restaurant or your suite?" Jonesy asked.

"In my suite," I replied. "If we dine in the restaurant, I'm sure Miss Dawson will attempt to join us. The longer we avoid her, the more she'll realise I will not be moved on this matter."

As soon as the elevator doors opened, I breathed a sigh

of relief. The day seemed to drag from the moment I awoke. I knew why, of course. Being away from Tess had left me feeling anxious and at odds with the world. Nothing seemed to go to plan, apart from the meeting with the Saudis. Prince Amir was an intelligent, knowledgeable businessman, as well as being extremely entertaining. I've always enjoyed his company and often spend time with him socially whenever we are in the same country. He'd heard about my marriage to Tess and had brought her a gift: an emerald tennis bracelet in a gold setting. A beautiful, timeless piece, though I fear it might be a little too heavy for my wife's delicate wrists.

Heading straight to the drinks cabinet, I poured myself a vodka. I needed to kick back a little, relax, and shake away the stress of all the political crap that hankered my attempts to meet with Eitan Harel. I needed…her. My beautiful, innocent, beguiling Tess. The woman who held my heart and soul in a grip so tight I could barely breathe without seeing her smile or hearing her soft voice and unrestrained laughter. I wanted to hold her hand and kiss those delicate fingers, but I had to settle for tapping into the security system in my home and accessing the live camera feeds.

Tess, Ivan, Kevin, Jack, Nan, and Jean sat at the kitchen table playing Monopoly. The board had belonged to James when he was a child. I would often find James, Catherine, and Nan playing the property game when I came home. Of course, James would always insist on being the banker so he could sneak a little extra money whenever he paid someone for passing go. Catherine pretended not to notice, but she would steal an extra hotel or two to strip him of his ill-gotten gains.

I'd mentioned it to Catherine's father and jokingly asked if their devious business acumen came from him. He'd just smiled and told me it was the Lassiter way and that, for him, the game could never be over until he owned the whole board. My father-in-law had been an extremely successful property magnate and was well-respected in the hotel industry. And yet, in the years since he'd passed away, I'd also heard stories that painted him as a ruthless man with ties to less-than-honourable business associates. Nevertheless, he'd left his family an extremely profitable legacy that James and I were determined to see prosper.

From what I could view of the game, Nan appeared to be winning. Kevin picked up his phone and glanced at both the cameras in the kitchen with the barest hint of a smile. He knew I was watching. It took another twenty seconds for the audio to kick in, giving me an earful of my cousin complaining that Nan had cheated. It appeared that she had been lucky enough to follow in Lassiter's footsteps, buying hotels on Park Lane and Mayfair, as well as all four train stations. Tess was laughing at him, pointing out that he owned Coventry Street, Leicester Square, and Piccadilly, with a hotel on each. I agreed with Ivan when he said it wasn't what you owned but where you owned it that determined the game—whether that was on a Monopoly board or not.

Ivan owned property throughout Russia, along with a successful aviation company, though he wasn't interested in the business side of his profitable ventures. He'd been left a substantial inheritance from our grandfather on his passing, and being an only child, he'd also inherited his mother's entire estate. His father, Anton, had divorced my aunt two years before she died, yet he still tried to claim much of her estate, hiring a team of lawyers to act on his behalf. My father, who despised Anton, wasn't happy with that and made his thoughts on the matter clear, although Anton chose to ignore him…to his peril. They found his body in the Moskva River a week later. His friends and colleagues who'd worked alongside him in the theatres of Moscow mourned his loss, yet his son, who'd been living with us since his mother had passed, hadn't shed a single tear.

My father had always been extremely fond of Ivan and treated him like a son behind closed doors, though he distanced himself in public. It helped keep Ivan out of the Barinov Bratva business. A safety measure that let him lead a somewhat normal life.

There are many who cannot understand why Ivan, a multimillionaire in his own right, would want to work for me. I know he enjoys the flying, as well as Nan's cooking and mothering. But it's the camaraderie and sense of belonging that keeps him with me. Truth be told, the men in my team are like his family. The brothers he never had. He doesn't need the wage I pay him; he doesn't need to live alongside the rest of the ex-military men on my estate. Yet he chooses to do so. It makes him happy.

I heard Tess groan when she threw the dice and landed on the *Go to Jail* square. Everyone laughed as she blew out a heavy sigh and shook her head.

"As if I haven't spent enough time in police stations lately," she whined.

"At least you don't have to put up with those stupid detectives this time," Ivan commented.

"No, I just have to put up with you," Tess replied. She poked him in the chest and stuck out her tongue.

Ivan grabbed her hand, pulled her out of her chair, and picked her up before striding towards the door.

"Ivan, what are you doing? Put me down," she yelled as he tipped her upper body over his shoulder.

"I am getting you out of jail," he replied with a smirk she couldn't see.

I switched camera feeds and watched as he made his way to the pool.

"Don't you dare throw me in the pool," Tess shouted while beating at Ivan's solid, broad back.

He stood at the edge of the water and swung her around. Tess screamed with laughter and grabbed his T-shirt.

"If I'm going in, then you're coming with me," she told him.

Danny came into view with the little dog, Bess. Ivan tipped Tess upside down in front of him; his laughter bellowed around the sheltered pool area when Bess began licking Tess's face excitedly.

Once Ivan gave in to Tess's demands to place her on her feet, he ran from beside the pool towards the basketball courts with Tess hot on his heels. Their antics made me smile, though I couldn't help feeling slightly jealous. I wanted to be the one putting a smile on her beautiful face. I wanted to be the man who made her laugh so hard she could barely speak. I wanted to be her everything.

Instead of calling home to speak to Tess, I left her to have her fun with my cousin. She needed to let loose after the last few days. To be under so much stress wasn't good for anyone.

Chapter Twelve

KOLYA

It had taken two days for the Israelis to grant me a sit-down with Eitan Harel.

In an act of courtesy, I had allowed Caroline Dawson to accompany us on the flight to Israel, although I'd distanced myself with the excuse of having work to do, leaving Gustav to entertain her. Their conversations about various foreign affairs issues had become quite heated, and I'd been grateful when Marie, our flight attendant, interrupted their potentially volatile discussion when she'd arrived with refreshments.

We landed in Tel Aviv mid-afternoon and made the fifteen-mile journey into the city via bulletproof town cars that Gustav had secured.

Dense grey cloud obscured the sun, and the air was suffocatingly humid. I couldn't wait to remove my shirt and take a shower.

Jonesy voiced his displeasure at the sickening heat and said he'd never moan about the weather in England again.

Everyone looked at him and laughed. Jonesy always moaned about the weather, no matter the season. I appreciated the excuse to smile; it relieved some of the tension we all felt about the upcoming visit with the man involved in my assassination attempt.

Josef Aksamit apologised for the delay in arranging my meeting with Harel, although the apology did not roll off his tongue easily. It was clear to see that the minister was not so happy with the turn of events. Whether that was due to my withholding the sale of the system or Mossad denying me access to Harel, I could not be sure. But my assurance that the defensive armoury would be in Israeli hands by the end of the month made him breathe a little easier.

I had great respect for the Israeli people. Generally, they were a welcoming, courteous nation. Before my request to meet with Harel, the business I'd conducted with the representatives I'd met went smoothly, without issue.

Josef Aksamit voiced his concerns regarding future business. I assured the man I was happy to meet with him again. He seemed overly relieved. I wondered whether his reaction was because of another weapon his country was interested in. Gustav informed him that KOLCAT's portfolio of weaponry and defence aids would be available on request. Josef thanked us and then asked if we would join him for dinner this evening to discuss the terms of a possible future purchase. He seemed too eager for me to agree to dine with him, which concerned me.

Had he already spoken with Eitan Harel? Did he know what he was about to reveal?

I apologised, informing him I was flying back to England after meeting with Harel. I waited to see the disappointment he tried to mask before reassuring him that

Gustav would be happy to attend in my place, bringing our latest portfolio with him.

Eitan Harel sat in a high-backed leather armchair, drinking strong black coffee while staring out the window. He seemed unconcerned with our presence, his gaze never moving from the view of the busy street below. I could tell that Josef Aksamit was annoyed with the man's lack of respect, though I had expected it. The hitman wasn't happy that he'd been forced to meet me.

We were in a suite in the most luxurious hotel in Tel Aviv. I wondered if Eitan had chosen this venue as a *fuck you* to the Israeli government, as they'd be footing the bill. A glance to my left revealed a dining table filled with various half-eaten dishes; a bottle of Remy Martin Louis XIII Cognac sat on the coffee table in front of him.

His gaze flicked briefly to where my guards and I stood before moving back to the window again.

"I would prefer it if we lost the audience," he stated.

"My guards stay," I informed him. I turned to Josef Aksamit and told him he could wait outside. He could keep Caroline Dawson company. She'd made it her mission to follow us around the city.

When only Eitan, Jonesy, Nate, Donovan, and I remained, he gestured towards the sofa and asked if I would take a seat before offering me a cognac. I refused the drink, choosing to sit across from him yet away from the window. I would not leave myself open to a sniper's aim.

"Who hired you?" I asked, even though I knew he would not answer.

"How did you identify me?" he questioned. "I wore

facial prosthetics and a baseball cap. I am curious to know how you knew it was me."

I ignored his query and followed with a statement.

"I'm surprised you were the driver and not the shooter," I told him. I was determined to appear calm and impervious. I was anything but. I'd held my own against powerful men on more occasions than I care to remember, but being near this man tested my resolve.

Eitan turned to me, and with a smirk, he replied, "Who says I wasn't?"

For a moment, I was confused until Nate declared, "You took out the gunman?"

"Your guard is a clever man, Mr Barinov. But on the day in question, his skills as a bodyguard were somewhat lacking, if I recall."

To his credit, Nate did not show any reaction to Harel's disparaging words. His military training allowed him to keep his head when I would have more than likely shown anger if I were in his shoes. But then again, Nate knew he wasn't responsible for my lack of security that day. Yannis had his guards take lead protection as we left the building. A mistake my wife paid dearly for and one I will never make again.

"Will you give me the shooter's name?" I asked.

"He was an unknown. A Syrian refugee with some military training. No one of any significance."

"Yet you were hired to kill him. Why?"

"I do not question why, Mr Barinov. But money does not always buy discretion nor silence in those who are new to my line of work."

"So the bastard who hired you did not want me tracing the gunman back to him. Tell me, Mr Harel, was it shoot to kill? If that was so, I find it hard to believe that you were not the one taking aim."

Harel did not answer. He looked back out of the window for a moment as if deep in thought, then he glanced my way again and repeated his earlier question.

"How did you identify me?"

"Your watch," I replied, gesturing towards his wrist. Harel raised his eyebrows and then let out a short laugh.

"You should give whoever traced me through the watch a raise. They deserve it."

I leaned forward, making sure my eyes never left his.

"If you cannot give me a name, at least let me know if I should expect further attempts on my life. My wife took the bullet that was meant for me. I intend to keep her safe from further harm."

"You have nothing to fear from me, Mr Barinov. I was sorry to see the young woman injured. I saw how she leapt up to push you out of harm's way. Many people would have thought her collateral damage. I am not of that mind. My country has seen conflict for many years. Innocent people have been hurt or killed by being in the wrong place at the wrong time. I make it a point to ensure that the person on the receiving end of my bullet is the original target."

"You speak as if what you do is an honourable profession," I countered.

"Says the arms dealer," he scoffed.

"I told you about the watch; now you need to give me something in return. Or at least point me in the right direction," I reasoned.

He sat there wearing the same smirk he'd been sporting intermittently throughout our meeting, raising the bottle of cognac questioningly. I waited a few moments, and when he still did not answer, I got up to leave.

"One day, you may find that you have become a target,

like so many others before you. I hope I am alive to see that day. Only then will I raise a glass with you in mind," I stated before walking away.

When I reached the door, Harel called out, "*Et tu, Brute?*" before pouring himself another drink.

Chapter Thirteen

KOLYA

I tried to maintain a calm exterior, but on the inside, I was furious. Gustav had warned me about coming here to meet with Harel. He knew he would give very little away regarding the shooting. Hell, even I knew that. Yet I had to try. But what the fuck was his parting shot about?

Et tu, Brute? Did he think *I'd* be the one to kill him? Was he telling me to get in line while everyone else takes their turn? Or was he insinuating that *I* was Caesar? A powerful man with allies willing to turn on him in the most brutal way.

I meet with powerful men on a weekly basis and disappoint many of them when their bids are unsuccessful. In all the years I've been in business, I've turned down more offers than I care to remember.

Even though I usually deliver my weapons and armoury to the highest bidder, there are some political groups and countries whom I refuse to entertain. I have my team at KOLCAT research all interested parties, and those with connections to terrorism are immediately discounted. The same applies to any country engaged in civil war. Of course, they often have arms supplied by other governments that we deal with, so no matter how hard KOLCAT tries to uphold a moral or neutral stance, it does not mean that our weaponry or defence systems won't end up in the hands of those we aim to avoid.

Josef Aksamit waited in the hallway with Gustav and Caroline Dawson. They appeared to be engaged in a friendly discussion, though all but Gustav viewed me with slight apprehension when I strode past them.

"Mr Barinov?" Josef said my name as if asking a question he did not want the answer to. I paused and took a deep breath before turning back to him with a forced smile.

"I would like to thank you for your time and hospitality, Mr Aksamit. Unfortunately, I have received an urgent call and must leave immediately," I told him while shaking his hand.

"Then I wish you a safe journey, Mr Barinov, and hope that you will visit us again soon," he replied.

"Is there room for one more on your flight back to London?" Caroline Dawson asked. She gave me a confident smile, thinking I wouldn't refuse her in front of our Israeli host.

"There's plenty of room for those wishing to fly to Moscow with me, Miss Dawson," I replied in all seriousness. I watched as surprise showed for just a second on Gustav's face. He schooled his features well before saying, "Let me know how it goes."

"Is everything all right?" Caroline asked. Her expression showed concern, but I knew her well enough to realise she was fishing for information to feed back to her colleagues. My father was on quite a few watch lists— including Interpol and the FBI—and there are many who would find even the slightest scrap of information about him valuable.

Although I did not need to tell the inquisitive Miss Dawson anything, I decided it may benefit me to do so in this instance.

"I just found out that my friend had a heart attack last night, and I would like to see him before he has bypass surgery. It is also an excuse to visit both my family and the munitions plant while I am in the country."

I wasn't lying about my friend. Mikhail was admitted to the hospital late last night. It appeared his sixty-a-day habit and unhealthy lifestyle choices had finally taken their toll. But there was another reason why I did not want to be seen flying back to the UK. One that my anger and frustration with Eitan Harel had brought to the forefront of my mind.

Chapter Fourteen

KOLYA

It took two hours to get the flight plan changed from London to Moscow and another four hours until we landed in the city of my birth. During that time, I'd been making plans with both my security team in the UK and the men I'd taken to Israel with me.

Two of my guards, Dave and Gordon, had stayed in Yorkshire. They'd been liaising with a private investigator I employ, and he'd sent some information through this morning that I found particularly disturbing. He'd found another house in Nottingham that was being used by Hassan Akbar's uncle and several other men, three of whom were White British. Not only had they been taking in White British girls who looked to be from age twelve to eighteen, but they had also roughly bundled in a Muslim girl in traditional dress and hijab, who was sobbing hysterically. This surprised me. From what Farid Ali had said, they'd targeted White British girls because they were against their western way of living. However, from what Graham

Lacey, my PI, had discovered, these men also targeted Muslim girls whom they considered to be of a lower caste.

I know very little about the caste system—other than how grossly anti-religious it is. My good friend Imran has no tolerance for it. He and his family believe it has no place in Islam, yet it appears to be around in modern-day Britain's ever-growing Muslim population, where equality has little bearing among many of its own people.

I discussed with my PI how we could deal with this: how best to get the information to the police without giving away our involvement in the gathering of it. He told me he would make sure that the files would be on PC Foster's desk tomorrow morning, along with a copy sent to the nearest police station in Nottingham. It gave me just a short window of time in which to execute my plan.

———

"I trust you had an uneventful flight?"

It seemed strange to hear those words in Russian. I was so used to speaking English that my mother tongue seemed foreign to me now. Even Ivan and I conversed more in English of late.

My brother Yuri had been waiting for me in the private aircraft hangar our family uses in Moscow. He embraced me in a brotherly hug before patting me on the back and gesturing towards another Gulfstream 650 aircraft. Then he handed me the documents I'd requested.

"You will fly to Barcelona, where you will pick up a passenger, Manuel Tigas, before flying over to Leeds Bradford Airport in the UK. So, as far as anyone is aware, the flight originated in Spain. The return journey will be the same in reverse. You will fly from Leeds Bradford Airport to

Barcelona, then back to Moscow. You will be photographed tomorrow afternoon outside your munitions plant before joining us for dinner."

"Thank you, Yuri. You are as meticulous in your planning as ever. I only wish you could come and work for me," I told him with a genuine smile—the first one I'd worn all day.

"You could never afford me, Kolya. And I'm sure if your young wife were to see how good-looking I am in person, she'd realise she's married the wrong brother," he joked. I laughed along with him as we made our way to the plane.

"I cannot wait to introduce you to her in person. Video calling is a great way to keep in touch, but I feel the distance more as the years go by," I admitted.

Yuri stopped walking and took hold of my arm.

"I hope you are not implying that you wish to come back to Moscow, Kolya."

"No, Yuri, I could never do that. Yet none of us are getting any younger, and we see so little of each other. Less so now than we did before James began studying in the States. If I have a child with Tess, I want you and Aleksei to be a part of their life."

"Kolya, you made the right decision when you kept James away from Moscow. You know this. Seeing us just two or three times per year, although hard, was also a good decision. Do not change that if you are lucky enough to become a father again. Bratva need only be a word your children hear when they are older. It does not have to be their way of life."

"How is our father?" I asked when we approached the steps of the aircraft. "Does he know about any of this?"

"He knows your plane has landed; he does not know the

rest. He is attending a pre-arranged function tonight. I believe the president might also be attending, though I am willing to wager that Roman Barinov requires more security guards." Yuri chuckled before adding, "His paranoia regarding security has served him well over the years. He's one of the oldest pakhans in Moscow."

"Tell him I will see him tomorrow. And, Yuri, thanks again for arranging this. I'll explain everything in more detail when I return."

"I need no other explanation than you gave me earlier, Kolya. This is for my sister-in-law's safety. She is family. We do not tolerate those who threaten our own. On this, I am Barinov Bratva through and through."

Chapter Fifteen

KOLYA

Franco had been waiting in a specially procured vehicle outside Leeds Bradford Airport in West Yorkshire. Manuel Tigas—the wealthy property developer turned politician— had taken Nate along with him to a hotel in Leeds, where he was having dinner with a friend. They'd taken a separate car, leaving us plenty of time to get to Doncaster.

I wondered what kind of dirt Yuri and my father had on the seemingly mild-mannered Tigas. It must have been something substantial to make him fly to the UK with *three new bodyguards* at such short notice. But then again, property developers had taken some serious monetary hits since the recession, leaving many previously successful businessmen and women needing help from less than honourable sources. And, of course, the political arena has always been rife with corruption.

Passing through the private gates at the airport had been relatively easy. Not a single one of us had been asked for our passport—which can often happen on VIP flights. It was late in the evening, and as far as airport security was concerned, we'd been checked and cleared in Barcelona. I was glad of it. It was one less thing to worry about.

Franco had met with Rashid, Dave, and Gordon, making sure both the capture and detaining of Hassan Akbar had gone according to plan. It hadn't been easy. Since being questioned by the police, he'd had a family member with him constantly. Rashid had suggested we take Hassan outside his mosque—a place where our target would feel safe—but there was no way that Hassan would leave without a struggle. If we took him from there, he'd alert everyone around him. Although, there was something I had in my arsenal that could work in our favour.

In situations such as this, the Bratva often used scopolamine, or Devil's Breath, as it's more commonly known. In the correct dosage, the drug makes the recipient more compliant, in an almost zombie-like state. You can also use it as a kind of truth serum. My father had given it to me after I'd had problems with an information leak at one of my manufacturing plants. He told me I should use it on anyone I suspected might be responsible for the leak, thereby ridding myself of the untrustworthy employee. Of course, as a respectable businessman, I would never do that —not while abiding by the laws of the country I call home. But as an overprotective husband and the youngest son of a Russian mafia king, I would do whatever the fuck I wanted.

The drug doesn't show up in any toxicology screening and is administered without an injection. You just need to get your target to breathe it in.

Wearing a traditional thobe, Rashid followed Hassan and his uncle into the mosque. Hassan had been alone for barely ten seconds before Rashid approached him, professing to be Farid Ali's cousin with news of his whereabouts. Hassan took him into a cloakroom so they wouldn't be overheard.

Rashid had previously emptied a small amount of the drug onto a thick cotton cloth, which he thrust in Hassan's face, holding it over his nose while he struggled to pull it away. If Rashid hadn't possessed such brute strength, our target could have wrestled the cloth away and would not have inhaled enough to leave him susceptible to our suggestions.

When he was sure the drug had taken effect, Rashid removed the cloth and wrapped it inside the surgical glove he'd worn. He told Hassan he should leave the mosque with him, and that there was a vehicle waiting for them outside. At first, Hassan seemed almost catatonic and was unsteady on his feet, but after a minute, he could stand unaided. Rashid steered him towards an emergency exit, where he called for Franco to collect them. And now here we all were in Fellbrook Woods, Doncaster, next to the boggy marsh where Sarah Crowther's battered, decaying body was discovered.

"Do you remember me?" I asked the bound, prone man after Jonesy dumped him on the ground in front of me.

Hassan Akbar looked my way, his face a mix of anger and confusion. He was still a little groggy from the drug, but that was wearing off fast—the fear and adrenaline helping to purge his body of the narcotic substance.

I delivered a swift, hard kick to his flabby stomach before asking the same question once again. "Do you remember me?"

"You were there the night that ginger-haired bitch threw a plant pot at my uncle's car. I recorded it, and I've shown the police."

"I'm sure you have, Mr Akbar. I have also shown them

footage of that very same night when you came to Jean Brent's house hoping to intimidate my wife, or to get her to retaliate—incriminating herself in the process."

"I don't even know your wife, so what the fuck are you on about? I didn't do anything wrong. That mad ginger bitch attacked *us*."

"The mad ginger bitch you are referring to is my wife, Tess Barinov—formally known as Tess Robertson. I do not wish to hear her spoken about in such a derogatory manner again. Is that clear?"

He did not answer, so I kicked him again—hard enough to hear at least two ribs break and leave him gasping for breath. I wished my Italian leather brogues were steel-capped so I could inflict more damage.

"Over the last three months, I've had a PI investigate you and your friends. I've been receiving detailed reports from them weekly. My PI thinks we have enough written and photographic evidence to enable the police to take immediate action. It will be delivered to the local stations, both here and in Nottingham, in a matter of hours. I would assume that since your name appears so often in those reports, the police will make it their priority to take you back in for questioning and keep you under surveillance. Although a part of me would like to see that happen, Mr Akbar, it would have made it so much harder to capture and kill you. As it stands, your last known whereabouts is the mosque we took you from. We were lucky that the area around the mosque has limited CCTV. It meant that my tech experts had very few cameras to disable. If only it had been that easy when we captured and killed your friend Farid Ali."

"Farid is dead?" He almost screamed out the question,

understanding his situation would end the same way. "I thought he'd gone to one of his cousins in Pakistan."

"Is that where your brother is? With one of *your* cousins?" I asked. So far, my efforts to find the elusive Tariq Akbar had come to nothing. This information might make things a little easier.

"I could spend a lot of time torturing you tonight," I told him. "I have imagined many ways in which I could inflict pain upon your wretched body. Unfortunately, I have a flight to make in less than an hour. Therefore, your death will have to come much swifter than I had planned."

I turned slightly, gesturing to the man behind me. "Rashid, hand me my gun."

"What? No, please. Whatever you think I've done, you have it all wrong," Hassan yelled, slowly getting up onto his knees—the pain from his ribs evident in his face with every movement he made.

"I doubt that very much, Mr Akbar. I obtained a confession from Farid Ali before his death, and I have the evidence from my PI and information from my wife."

"They're lying! I've done nothing wrong," he cried.

"Are you calling my wife a liar? You, a murdering paedophile?" I yelled before kicking him in the balls as hard as I could. He let out a loud cry that turned into a groan as he fell forward onto his face. Rashid, Jonesy, and Franco winced simultaneously and put their hands over their crotches. A reaction that seems pre-programmed into all men from an early age. After all, a kick to the balls is never forgotten.

When Hassan had finally stopped crying, I crouched down beside him. Grabbing a fistful of hair, I raised his head, pressing the muzzle of my Beretta 9mm between his bloodshot eyes.

"You have a habit of trying to scare people by making a gun shape with your hand—as if you will come back and shoot them when they least expect it. I thought it was only a scare tactic at first, but my PI has photographic evidence of you—alongside two of your friends—buying several rifles and shotguns from the boot of a car. You were trading what appeared to be a package containing drugs, though my PI couldn't get close enough to confirm it.

"You tried to intimidate Tess outside Jean Brent's house, and as a parting shot, you made your hand into the make-believe gun shape you are so fond of. Ironically, Mr Akbar, Tess had recently married me," I explained with a sardonic smile, "...a developer and distributor of weaponry the likes of which you can only imagine. I can disassemble a gun with my eyes closed quicker than you can get your zipper down to take a piss. So all your threat did was make me want to shoot you myself. But then I had a conversation with my wife. She was upset with me, and with anger and frustration, she admitted she wanted to bash your skull in with something hard and heavy. Tess wanted you to suffer the same injuries as her foster sister, Sarah Crowther, leaving your body to rot in a boggy marsh."

"Please. I have a family. People who rely on me. My mother is disabled and—"

"Sarah had a family, too. A foster mother and sister who loved her dearly. She had a life to live. You had no thought for her or any of the other girls you murdered."

Hassan protested his innocence while pleading for his life, but his words meant nothing to me.

"Farid Ali was exceedingly forthcoming with information after he sustained a harsh beating. I have to say...he took longer than you did to cry and beg. How does that make you feel, Mr Akbar? Knowing your friend was much braver in the face of his impending death than you."

"Please don't shoot me. Farid's a liar. It was him that killed Sarah," Hassan whined.

"Oh, I'm not going to shoot you. I promised Tess she would get her wish, and a husband should honour every promise he makes to his wife." I handed the gun back to Rashid and asked Franco to pass me the item I'd had him buy before leaving Oxford.

The concrete plant pot was large—almost a foot long—and was extremely heavy. It took great effort to swing it at Hassan's head. The first blow to his temple did little but knock him to the ground. He'd seen it coming and had tried to get away, but there was nowhere he could go. Though the weather had been exceptionally warm, the marsh was still boggy. Hassan's knees sank into the wet earth, leaving him no room to manoeuvre. I struck him again with more force this time, hearing both a dull thud and then a crack as his skull caved in. I hit him five more times with the heavy pot, twice in the side of his head and three times in his face, leaving him an unrecognisable, bloody mess. Once I'd finished, Franco handed me a black refuse sack, where I placed the bloody plant pot. He tied the top of the sack and put it back in the boot of the car.

Some might question my choice of murder weapon, but I thought it was fitting. It was my wife's weapon of choice just a week ago, so in a way, I felt it only right that I should honour the choice she made.

After donning gloves, Jonesy and Rashid each took hold of two long branches, which they used to push Hassan's body further into the marsh. Moving him wasn't an effortless task. Though he wasn't tall, the man had a stocky build, and his dead weight was hard to shift. I usually have a strong stomach, but seeing Hassan's brains and the back of his skull left behind as my men rolled him away made me gag.

"Boss, if you're going to throw up, do it in a bag in the car. You don't want to leave DNA evidence here," Franco said. His tone was very matter-of-fact, as if what he saw didn't bother him.

All the men with me tonight had seen active combat and had no doubt witnessed bodies in much worse states than this—some of those being people they had served alongside. Friends, even.

Jonesy and Rashid made their way back to dry, hard ground as carefully as possible, using the branches to scrape over any footprints left on the soft, muddy ground before throwing them into the wettest part of the marsh.

While Franco made sure we'd left nothing behind, the rest of us got into the vehicle. I could sense Rashid was troubled over what we'd done. If he'd not read the file of evidence collected by my PI and his team, I don't think he'd have suggested going to the mosque to take Hassan.

He wasn't the only one disturbed by what he'd read. I'd shared the information with most of my team, and we'd all concluded that, although there were many good police officers out there—such as PC Foster and her colleague, PC Winters—some just couldn't be trusted.

My PI had uncovered information regarding the previous imam of the mosque Hassan Akbar had frequented. He'd been accused of abusing young boys aged between seven and nine who attended the mosque. This had been happening for several years until two of the boys he abused alerted someone. There had been a meeting in which the boys' family members decided to keep the matter quiet, so the boys wouldn't grow up being known as victims of abuse. A stigma they feared would blight their chance at a normal life. But as more children came forward, it became clear they couldn't hide it from the authorities any longer.

The imam was arrested and taken to the police station for questioning, but he disappeared after being released. On further investigation by my PI, he found that Chief Inspector Carrick had approved his release not even twenty-four hours after two of the boys had made incriminating statements.

Being ex-police, my PI thought this was an odd move, so he looked for a connection between Carrick and the imam. He discovered the imam was a member of the golf club that Carrick and the detectives my wife calls Dickhead and Twatface belong to. It also transpired that the imam sold his house to Carrick two days after his release for less than half the price of its current value.

If that doesn't scream corruption, then my father is a saint.

"Rashid, I know that your part in what we did tonight will weigh heavily on your conscience—especially the religious aspect of taking him from a place of worship. So, if you need time away from your employment, I am more than happy to grant that with full pay."

He cleared his throat before replying, "Thanks, boss. I'm taking Julie and the kids away for a few days anyway, so I'll have time to process then."

He looked directly at me, the glow from the vehicle's interior light highlighting his glassy eyes. "This guy needed taking out. He and the imam are a disgrace to all that is true Islam. I don't understand why the families of those boys didn't want the imam to suffer. If he'd have touched my children, I'd have ripped him apart with my bare hands."

"Fear!" stated Jonesy as he placed his hand on Rashid's shoulder. "Just as it was when all that came out about the Catholic priests. They feared repercussions from the church, the community, and others who worshipped. And God Himself, of course. Those who prayed and devoted their lives to God feared for the place they thought they'd secured in heaven.

"Religions wield power," Jonesy added. "People have gone to war over them. Places of worship were embossed with gold and other riches while ordinary folk around them suffered and starved. They are all the same, Rashid. They've been that way forever."

"But you believe in God," Rashid pointed out. "You wear a crucifix. How can you think that way and still call yourself a Catholic?"

Shrugging his shoulders, Jonesy replied, "It's like anything else, I suppose. You pick and choose what aspects of religion you want to believe in. Take the Bible, for instance. It's there to teach us right from wrong, using various stories and verses from when the Romans sought to conquer the world.

"Now you and me," Jonesy said, gesturing between him and Rashid. "We enjoy reading. Always have done. But if we sat down and talked about a book we'd read and enjoyed, each of us could have taken something different from the story. The chapters that stand out for one of us might not be what stands out for the other. That's how I see religion. You take something good that appeals to you about it and ignore the rest—the stuff you think is utter bullshit and has no bearing on your life or the world in the here and now.

"I believe in heaven. Not necessarily what everyone else believes in, but I like to think there's a place I can go where

I'll see my mam again, along with all my other friends and family who've passed before me. I believe in love and kindness, and respecting others. I believe in defending people who can't, for whatever reason, defend themselves. That's why I joined the army, and it's what we've done tonight—although on a smaller, more personal scale. That bastard out there in the marsh had raped and murdered young girls. He'd ruined the lives of so many and would have carried on doing so. And if I could get my hands on that so-called imam, I'd kill him too. The police seem to do fuck all, and the kids don't stand a chance at defending themselves if no one in authority will listen. So for all the scumbags involved, we are the authority. We've listened and have taken appropriate action. Case closed."

"Wow, Jonesy! I don't know what to say to all that. It was all very…profound," declared Rashid with notes of awe and humour in his voice.

"I have my moments," Jonesy replied with a smirk. "How long's Franco going to be? I'm fucking starving."

"How can you have an appetite after what's just happened?" I asked, dumbfounded.

"We've had nothing but fancy-cut sandwiches today, and tiny cakes that would have left a midget hungry. Once we get out of Doncaster, send Rashid to a takeaway for kebab and chips," he replied.

"We'll have plenty of food waiting for us when we get to Moscow," I told him.

"Boss, not being funny, but you Russians have a habit of pickling everything. Whatever dish I order, you can bet there's pickled fucking cabbage on the side to spoil it."

I laughed out loud at his words and the grimace he wore before replying, "Says the man who just requested kebab and chips."

Chapter Sixteen

TESS

It had been twelve long days since I last saw Kolya in person. I'd spoken to him daily over the phone, and we'd video-called every other day. He appeared a little preoccupied with whatever work he was dealing with, and being around his father didn't seem to help matters.

Kolya was always wary whenever his father asked to speak to me. He'd told me about Roman's position within the Russian mob, but honestly, the man had been nothing but charming and funny whenever I'd spoken to him. I asked Kolya if it would be okay to accompany him the next time he travelled to Russia, but all he said was, "We'll see."

We had to go to an event at some posh place in Park Lane tonight, so Kolya had Ivan fly me to London to meet him at his hotel. He'd arranged for me to get my hair and make-up done at the spa, and last week Nan had taken Jean and me to the shop where I bought my wedding dress to pick out a suitable gown for the event. I chose a long emerald-green strapless dress that had to be taken up to fit, yet it still skimmed the floor even though I wore high heels. I had a black chiffon wrap that draped across my shoulders and a black and green clutch bag that cost almost as much as the dress. My days of scrimping and saving my pittance of an allowance seemed like another lifetime ago.

My hair and make-up were amazing. I looked older and kind of sophisticated, like I deserved to be on the arm of a man like Kolya. I couldn't wait for him to see me. Danny and Franco were blown away when they saw my transformation, although Franco told me I always looked beautiful, whether I wore fancy clothes and make-up or not. Danny agreed, then took me in his arms and began twirling me around before dancing around the room with me.

I was breathless and giggling by the time Kolya arrived, so I didn't see him at first. But even before our eyes met, I knew he was there. It's like something happens to the air in the room when he enters. A strange kind of awareness takes over me. My heartbeat doubles, and my senses seem sharper.

I turned to look at him, taking in his rumpled appearance, which was most unlike the man I married. "Are you okay?" I asked as I walked towards him.

"It was a long flight," he murmured before reaching out to touch my hair. He ran his hand along my collarbone, stopping at the scar from the bullet wound. I'd purposely left my hair down to cover it, but as always, Kolya zeroed in on it with a frown.

"You can hardly see it, Kolya. With the tan and my hair, I'm sure no one will notice. I thought I looked nice. Everyone else seems to think so," I said defensively.

"My darling, you are the most beautiful woman I've ever seen," he stated. "I shall be the envy of every man in the building."

He trailed his hand down my chest, over my breasts and

down my arms until he came to my hands, which he lifted to his mouth. He kissed each finger individually before turning my hand to cup his cheek.

"Kolya," I whispered. The warmth from his delicate touch spread throughout my whole body, heightening the pulsating need in my core. I licked my lips—my mouth feeling dry despite drinking a glass of water not five minutes before.

To my utter disappointment, Kolya let go of my hand and stepped away from me.

"I need to take a shower and get ready. The drive from the airport took longer than expected."

"Do you need any help?" I asked, raising my eyebrows suggestively. I watched his eyes widen in surprise before he snapped, "No, I don't." Then he turned and made his way to his room.

I lifted my gown, walked over to the sofa, and then sat for a few minutes, wondering where the Kolya from twelve days ago had disappeared to. The one who'd kissed me so passionately and gave me my first orgasm. The one who'd held me all night when I'd been angry and upset.

The man who'd told me he loved me.

Chapter Seventeen

KOLYA

With shaking hands, I poured myself a brandy, hoping to calm the raging beast inside me—the one who wanted to bring my wife in here and take her up on what she offered.

She looked so incredibly beautiful—a goddess in green satin. The colour complemented her coppery curls, which gleamed like silk under the light.

How did I not think she would affect me after all this time?

I wanted to tear the dress from her body and take her hard against the wall. Virginity be damned. Tess is temptation itself. My very own Eve. Yet it is she who is the forbidden fruit I am not allowed to bite.

I undressed in haste, stepping into the shower to wash away the feelings of frustration that powered through my veins like some enhanced drug. Less than five minutes in her presence and I already knew the situation was hopeless. There were just three weeks left until her eighteenth birthday, that's all. Surely it should be easier to maintain my self-imposed sexual abstinence than this? I am not some errant teenager ruled by raging testosterone. I am a man in my prime with control over how and when I bed a woman.

Sighing heavily, I took hold of the throbbing erection that tapped against my belly. Who was I kidding? I was no more in control around Tess than a pubescent teen experiencing his first wet dream.

As I brought myself to an unfulfilling climax, I knew the next few weeks would be hell on earth for me.

The short drive to the venue was uneventful. Tess seemed nervous; I took her hand in mine to stop her fidgeting. Not ten seconds later, her foot began tapping repeatedly on the floor of the car, so I placed my free hand on her knee to quell the movement. She leaned into me and sighed before saying, "I really missed you. I wish we were at home watching Netflix right now."

"Tess, tonight is very important for KOLCAT. Among the attendees is a French ambassador. He has significant influence on how speedily items can be brought to the table to be considered by the European Parliament. Monsieur Alleman is a member of the EU council and is already aware of my interests in purchasing land in the Czech Republic."

"What does the European Parliament have to do with it?" she asked, her brow furrowed. "Surely you just need to buy the land from whoever's selling it?"

"Usually, that is exactly what we would do, but the EU can waive some of the taxes and levies imposed on such a buy. If you are willing to bring a successful business to an EU country in need of economic regeneration, they make sure the rewards are financially beneficial."

"So we have to do a bit of schmoozing tonight!" she stated with a smile.

"My darling, the only thing *you* have to do is be yourself. But yes, these types of events are all about the schmoozing, as you so eloquently put it. Informal conversations with powerful acquaintances—a few words in the right ear, so to speak. Successful ventures are often born of polite chat and vintage champagne."

"So you look like you're out to party, yet you're really out to work."

"That's exactly it, my love. Even in a tuxedo, I am KOLCAT. Though I promise we'll make time to dance and enjoy our evening."

Jonesy and Franco exited the Range Rover in front of us and came to stand by our car when we stopped. Nate got out first and stood to the right side of the passenger door that Tess and I emerged from. Jonesy would be guarding me tonight while Nate minded Tess. I felt she would be more comfortable with Nate doing close protection detail. They seemed to have struck up an easy friendship, and I trusted he would step in to act as both guard and advisor if we were separated for any reason. Franco will be positioned near the doorway of the great room, and Lucas will remain in the Mercedes, ready to pick us up should we need to leave quickly.

Dave and Gordon were already in the venue's foyer: an old yet recently refurbished government building on Park Lane. I'd been here plenty of times over the years in the guise of raising money for various charities. But even though those worthy causes benefitted from our gatherings, as with most philanthropic events, the real reason behind them was business. To some, just being seen amongst the powerful of our social elite was worth the substantial charitable donation expected of every attendee.

On entering the grand room, we were met by Rupert Langley, the Secretary of State for Foreign and Commonwealth Affairs, and Richard Havendale, Secretary of State for Defence. Both men were important to KOLCAT, and for that very reason, I greeted them warmly, shaking their hands before introducing my wife. Tess's reaction almost mimicked their own. She stood there open-mouthed, no doubt recognising both the government ministers from TV and newspapers.

After an awkward few seconds, Rupert Langley shook my hand again, congratulating me loudly, causing quite a few people to glance our way. He took Tess's hand in his and kissed the back of it, declaring me a lucky man to have such a beautiful young wife. With emphasis on the young. Something neither I nor his wife—who was standing just a few steps away—was happy to hear. Richard Havendale also took Tess's hand, his lips lingering slightly longer than both Tess and I were comfortable with. I didn't hear the congratulatory words he uttered; I was too busy fighting the urge to throat-punch the bastard for his audacity.

I placed my hand on the small of Tess's back possessively, giving as few details as possible about our wedding before politely excusing us so we could leave the lecherous male. His covetous stare boiled my blood, but to make my feelings clear would have severe repercussions.

Telling Richard Havendale he'd look a damn sight better with a bullet between his eyes was something I doubt he'd appreciate.

Attaching his photograph to the targets I use in my gun range would have to do instead. I could print more than a dozen and make a morning of it, firing enough rounds into his image to obliterate his weasel-like features.

I took two glasses of champagne from the tray of a server and handed one to my wife. Tess had a couple of glasses of wine at our wedding, but she rarely drank at home, even though there was always wine with our meal and a selection of spirits on display. She suffered from migraines and said she didn't want to do anything that could bring on a headache. Still, she downed the champagne in one go, probably trying to give herself some Dutch courage—enough to deal with the room full of strangers she found herself facing.

"Take it easy with the champagne, my love. If you keep drinking it like that, it will go straight to your head," I remarked when a server replaced her empty glass with a full one.

"I think I need it, Kolya. I've seen those two blokes on the telly. They're government ministers. And you are friends with them."

"I wouldn't call us friends, Tess. More like…acquaintances, shall we say. Langley, I can tolerate, but Havendale is a—"

"Prick!" she stated, before downing half her second glass of champagne with a grimace. "I thought it would taste better the more I drank, but it's just…bitter."

I smiled at her description. To the inexperienced palate, I could understand that the taste might take some getting used to.

"My darling, at around two hundred and fifty pounds per bottle, I doubt the hosts would appreciate you proclaiming it bitter," I declared with a smirk.

"TWO HUNDRED AND FIFTY QUID?" she

exclaimed a little too loudly, garnering us a great deal of attention.

"Shh," I whispered. "Remember where we are, my love."

"Sorry," she said. The flush of embarrassment was clear to see despite her skilfully applied makeup. "You just shocked me, Kolya. The servers have around a dozen glasses on each tray. How many bottles does that equate to? Will they keep serving it all night?"

"Of course. There's also a bar through those double doors over there, although it's quite unnecessary—a server will bring you any liquor you request—but often men like to congregate around a bar as the evening progresses."

"It all seems a bit much to me. I mean, there are so many homeless people sleeping rough on the streets of London, not knowing when they'll be able to afford their next meal, while people here are drinking fizzy, fermented grape juice at two hundred and fifty quid a pop. Can't you see how wrong that is?"

She was right, of course. Yet that was the way of the world I belonged to. Her world now, whether she was comfortable with it or not.

"My darling, we can discuss the rights and wrongs of this event later," I told her while guiding her further into the room. "I must speak to Monsieur Alleman before he leaves. Let us find him so I can see how amenable he is to my proposal; then, we can take advantage of the orchestra and dance the night away."

Chapter Eighteen

TESS

I hated every minute I'd been in this place. Here I was, dressed to the nines, make-up and hair making me look like I belonged on a magazine cover, yet the confidence I thought my appearance would give me fled as soon as I got in the car. And now everyone was looking at me, judging me. Judging Kolya, too.

The few conversations I'd had over the last hour hadn't helped matters. Where did we meet? How long had we known each other? What did I do for a living?

I could hardly tell them the truth, though the lies that rolled off my tongue became more elaborate with each glass of champagne that passed my lips. After three glasses of bubbly, I'd turned into a veritable Barbara Cartland, with Kolya as my dashing romantic hero.

With the fourth glass of champagne, I realised that the taste had changed, and I was actually enjoying it. It even quelled the hunger I felt.

Kolya had been talking to the French fella for the last

forty minutes, and I was bored out of my mind. I wished I'd gone to see *Mamma Mia* in the West End with Ivan.

I hadn't realised that Kolya could speak French—or that most of their conversation would be in French. I picked up the odd word here and there, but they spoke so fast, and I was completely clueless as to how well it was going for my determined hubby.

Hearing him speak French so fluently really did something for me. It was the same whenever he was speaking to Ivan in Russian.

Kolya looked so sexy tonight in his tux. He filled a suit out so well that it was almost a crime for him to wear anything else. I'd seen quite a few women giving him a bit more than an appreciative glance, and while I really couldn't blame them, I didn't like it one bit.

I turned to Nate, telling him I needed the ladies' room. I probably could have waited a bit longer, but I needed a change of scenery, and my high heels were killing me. I'd spent the last two weeks in trainers or flip-flops, so my feet were screaming to be set free from their torturous, expensive prisons.

When I wobbled a little on the way to the bathroom, Nate looped his arm through mine and whispered, "No more champagne for you, sweetheart. You aren't used to it."

"I'm not drunk," I protested. Pointing down towards my feet, I continued, "It's the shoes. They're too high."

"Right," he said with a smirk as we stopped in front of the bathroom door. He glanced at Franco, who I had to admit was looking mighty fit tonight. Franco nodded back, so Nate let go of my arm and gestured for me to go ahead.

I opened the door expecting to find a row of toilet cubicles, so you can imagine my surprise when I was greeted by what appeared to be a lounge, complete with a sofa and chairs. Opposite them, a long ornate gilt mirror sat above a row of sinks that rested in cream-coloured marble. A set of double doors later and I finally found the toilets. I'd almost turned around, thinking I'd gone to the wrong place.

Once I'd straightened my dress, I made my way out to the mirrored room. It was cooler in here, which helped clear my head a little. I'd been lying to Nate; I knew I was tipsy. My eyes looked slightly glassy, and I swayed a little when I leaned towards the mirror to apply more lipstick.

Satisfied with my appearance, I made my way back to Nate, trying my best to walk in a straight line.

"I think you should switch to water for the rest of the night, Tess," he said as we made our way back to Kolya.

"Excellent suggestion, Nate. Is it me, or has it suddenly got warmer?"

"No, that's just the alcohol hitting you. You aren't used to drinking, Tess, especially champagne. You should have paced yourself."

"I thought it was crap at first, but it's not bad at all once you've had a few," I told him.

"I'm sure you're right, sweetheart."

I stumbled a little and turned to face him when he caught me. He looked so suave and handsome in his fancy suit. He and Kevin made a lovely couple. I suddenly felt an overwhelming urge to tell him how much he meant to me. It came from out of nowhere, and I couldn't hold it in.

"I love you, Nate. And Kevin. You and Danny and Ivan are like my best friends in the whole world. Franco and Jonesy, too. I love you all."

"And we all love you too, Tess," he said while trying to

get me to start walking again. "But I think we need to find your husband before the alcohol makes you profess your love to anyone else."

"You don't believe me," I declared loudly.

"Honey, I do believe you. But I think your husband probably misses you right now, so we need to find him, okay?" His tone was half humorous, half pleading.

"My husband," I said with a giggle. "Can you believe it, Nate? I'm actually a married woman."

"Boss, I think your wife might need a glass of water," Nate said as we came to a stop in front of Kolya. He was standing next to a pretty blonde woman in a figure-hugging red dress. Her left hand was pressed against the lapel of his jacket.

"Are you all right, Tess?" Kolya asked.

I didn't reply. I was too busy glaring at the blonde bitch who thought she could touch my husband.

"Why don't you introduce us, Kolya?" the woman practically purred.

"Caroline, this is Tess, my wife. Tess, this is Caroline Dawson; she is—"

"Touching you," I pointed out calmly.

Kolya moved slightly, as if to shrug the woman's hand away, but all she did was loop her arm through his and lean into him.

"Pleased to meet you, Tess. Kolya didn't mention you when he took me to Israel last week. But then again, he kept me rather busy when we bumped into each other in Berlin."

Kolya rolled his eyes, but he didn't deny it.

"Your husband is a hard man to satisfy, Mrs Barinov. He always has been," she said while flicking an imaginary piece of lint from his shoulder.

I saw red. Anger and jealousy swept through my whole body at an alarming rate. My vision blurred a little— whether through alcohol or rage, I had no idea, but at that moment, all I could think of was pulling the bitch off him.

"Get your hands off my husband, you skank," I ordered.

"Excuse me?" she said, although she let go of Kolya.

"Tess, Caroline, that's enough," Kolya declared. He moved next to me and placed his hand on my arm. I shrugged him off and stepped towards the woman.

"If I see you touching any part of my husband again, you will live to regret it. Do I make myself clear?"

"How dare you speak to me like this? Do you know who I am?" she questioned, brushing off my words as if I was no one.

"Yes, you're a skank!" I stated.

"I'm the American attaché to—"

"So you're a Yank skank. So what?" I yelled. "I don't care whether you're American, British, or from Timbuk-fuckintu. If you touch my husband again, I'll—"

Before I could do or say anything more, Kolya grabbed me from behind, pinning my arms against my sides.

"Get off me, Kolya, you—"

"If you know what's good for you, Tess, you'll shut your fucking mouth and walk out of here quietly," Kolya whispered in my ear angrily. I looked around and realised almost everyone in the room was staring our way. At me in particular.

I felt as though I was split into two halves. One half wanted to yell, *What are you lot staring at?* while the other half wanted to curl up and hide. In the end, the decision was made for me. Franco stood in front of me, Nate to the side—effectively blocking the skank from my view. Kolya let go of my arms yet stayed behind me, with Jonesy keeping up the rear of our procession as we left the venue.

Chapter Nineteen

TESS

Franco held the car door open while Nate helped me inside. The fresh air had hit me hard. I felt like the earth had tilted somehow because my vision had suddenly distorted. I closed my eyes for a moment and took a deep, steadying breath before opening them. Everything was the right way up again, although I still felt a little queasy.

Kolya hadn't followed me into the car, and that didn't sit well with me. He could be talking to her: the skank. I wanted to scream and yell at him; to call him out on his cheating and deceit. The anger I'd kept a lid on when we'd made our exit began to build again. Fucking dirty, rotten, fickle men. They were all the same. Kolya had just proven that. It didn't matter if they were rich or poor, married or single. None of them could be trusted because they were all led by their dicks.

I glanced out of the window to find Kolya storming down the steps of the venue. He looked furious.

"Tess, I heard what Miss Dawson said in there, and I know how it sounded, but I swear to you, she was just being a bitch. Nothing happened between her and the boss." Nate sounded sincere, but I didn't want to hear it. I didn't feel like I could trust anyone at that moment. He was a man, after all. Lies seemed to roll off their tongues so easily, especially the one getting into the car beside me.

Lucas pulled the car away from the curb as soon as Kolya had closed the door. I turned my face towards the window, away from his angry glare. Streetlights and billboards gave a peaceful ambient glow to the luxurious interior—a complete opposite to the oppressive, turbulent atmosphere our combined ire created.

Neither of us said a word. My hands were shaking from the amount of restraint I needed not to lash out at him—and at the world in general—for the cruel twist in the hand I'd been dealt.

I thought I'd found happiness, love, and loyalty; I believed they could be mine for always. I should have known better. That would never be on the cards for someone like me.

When we arrived at the hotel, Nate got out and waited for Franco and Jonesy before opening the car door. Kolya got out first and reached inside to help me, ever the gentleman, even though he was livid with me. I avoided his helping hand like it was contaminated with some deadly disease. He said nothing, continuing to walk beside me as we entered the lift to the penthouse. Being here, in his space, made me feel slightly sick. Well, it was either that or the alcohol.

As soon as the door closed and we were alone, Kolya yelled, "Are you aware how much damage your outburst has caused tonight? Do you know how long it has taken me to get to this point with Monsieur Alleman? Only for your jealous tantrum to dissolve all the confidence and trust he had in my company."

"You want to talk about trust, Kolya? How about the trust I had in my husband not to fuck around with anyone while he was away on *business*?" I made sure I punctuated the word business with air quotes and a healthy dose of scepticism. Then I took off my shoes and threw them across the room.

"I had a valid reason to fly Caroline Dawson to Israel with me, but it wasn't so I could *fuck around* with her." He mimicked my air quotes when he said fuck around, which only served to infuriate me further.

"Does she work for you?" I asked as calmly as I could.

"No."

"Have you slept with her?"

"Yes, but that was a few years ago."

He answered as if it meant nothing to him, but his words sent a piercing pain through my heart.

"Then what reason would you have to meet her in Berlin and fly her to Israel with you?" I cried.

"So she could get me a meeting with Eitan Harel."

"And who the fuck is Eitan Harel?" I didn't recognise the name, but then again, Kolya told me very little lately.

"He was the man who drove the getaway car the shooter escaped in. We finally tracked him down, but he refused to see me. I threatened to pull out of a deal I was involved in with the Israelis, so Caroline Dawson got involved, and between her and an Israeli minister, I finally got my meeting."

I slumped down onto the sofa in shock, remembering everything that happened that day so clearly—the day I was shot saving Kolya's life.

"Why, Kolya? Why would you need to speak to him? For God's sake, he was involved in your assassination attempt. Why put yourself at risk?"

He walked over to the drinks cabinet and poured himself a scotch.

"I wanted to find the shooter and the one who arranged the hit. I need to know the threat has gone."

"And did you get that information?" I held my breath for the answer.

"The shooter is dead, and there is no threat from the driver. I knew before we spoke that he wouldn't give me a name, but I hoped..." He slammed his glass down on the cabinet, spilling whisky over the polished wood. "Et tu, Brute."

"Et tu, Brute?" I questioned.

"Those were his parting words. I threatened to pull out of a multimillion-dollar deal, pissed off a foreign government—and one of the world's most formidable intelligence agencies—and all I got was, *et tu, Brute.*"

"Why didn't you tell me, Kolya?"

"You couldn't deal with it, Tess. Look at you now, sitting there pale and shaking. Just thinking about that day fills you with dread."

"It doesn't matter, Kolya. You should have shared it with me. I'm your wife. We are supposed to be a team. We should support each other in something like this."

"Support?" he snapped. "I needed your support tonight at the event, and what did you do? You flew into a jealous rage, hurling insults in front of the very man I tried all night to gain favour from."

I jumped up from the sofa, my fear replaced by anger once again. My head swam, and my stomach churned, but I was determined to have my say.

"That woman had her hands on you. She was touching you like she had an intimate claim on you. She insinuated you'd had a dirty weekend together."

"It doesn't matter what *she* said or did. You shouldn't have acted the way *you* did. You're not in the foster home now, Tess. You can't go screaming at people and threatening them."

I huffed out a laugh. Did he honestly think I wouldn't have fought her? "Oh, believe me, Kolya, it wouldn't have been a threat. I'd have knocked her over-whitened teeth straight down her throat if she'd touched you again."

"You can't keep doing this, Tess. You must learn to act a certain way if you want to get anywhere in life. You need to have some semblance of control."

"You're nothing but a hypocrite, Kolya. Before we went in there tonight, you told me to just be myself. And let's talk about control, shall we? I believe it's what you nearly lost when that skeevy minister's lips were pressing against the back of my hand as he was eye-fucking me. I'm just glad you didn't see him fondle my boobs when I bumped into him on my way back from the loo."

It was a lie, of course. I just wanted to see his reaction.

"He did what?" he bellowed. "I'll fucking kill the bastard. Where was Nate? Why wasn't he protecting you?"

I laughed mockingly; I couldn't help myself. If Kolya could only see himself from the outside looking in.

"There he is. Mr Control. Calm and collected as always," I declared, gesturing towards him.

Within seconds, Kolya had me up against the wall, his face barely an inch from my own.

"Tell me you're lying. Tell me he didn't touch you that way," he demanded.

I could have carried on riling him up even further, but

having him this close, feeling his breath against my skin...it changed everything in an instant. Desire replaced feelings of anger and betrayal. It happened so quickly—like the flick of a switch. I had to be honest with him. For everyone's sake.

"Yes, Kolya, I lied. But now you know how I felt."

"You are playing a very dangerous game, *malyutka*. You would do well not to push me tonight. You might not like the outcome."

Malyutka. Little one. He'd stopped calling me that weeks ago. Is that how he still saw me? I couldn't have that. Not anymore.

I slipped my hand down to cup him through his trousers, feeling the outline of his length through the cloth.

"I'm not your little one, Kolya. I'm all woman. Your wife. I need you to be my husband. So make me yours. Prove that you want only me."

I thought I heard him growl before his lips crashed against mine. My head hit the wall with the sheer force of his hungry kiss. He thrust his tongue inside my mouth and flicked it against my own, causing me to whimper with unfulfilled need. I felt a throbbing between my legs, my underwear damp from arousal. This was going to happen. Tonight. Finally, I'd know how it felt to have him inside me.

Kolya's lips left mine to trail kisses across my jaw and throat, along with intermittent bites; his tongue soothing and beard tickling the sensitive areas his bites left behind. I was breathing hard and fast, wishing I was the same height as him so I could grind myself against his hardness—needing to feel some sort of friction to ease the ache that was building inside me. He bent a little, tugging the skirt of my dress up to my waist, then he lifted me up to bring my sex in line with his before rocking against me. After less than ten seconds, I was ready to come; my head swimming with the intensity of it.

Kolya fumbled with the front of his trousers just as the room began to spin. I felt like I was on a fairground ride—one that just wouldn't stop. My stomach churned, making me feel sick. I closed my eyes and tried to concentrate on what Kolya was doing, but the rocking of our bodies wasn't helping. He pulled my underwear to one side, and something brushed against me. I couldn't let this go any further, not when the champagne I drank was threatening to make an appearance.

"Kolya, no. You have to stop. Please," I panted. And thankfully, he listened, lowering me carefully to my feet before stepping away.

"I'm sorry, Kolya," I told him. I took a deep breath in, closing my eyes once again so I couldn't see the room spinning.

"Not as sorry as I am, malyutka."

I chanced opening my eyes, only to see him turn around and adjust his trousers.

"Kolya, you don't understand. It's the champagne, it—"

"Yes, of course. It made you brave. Made you feel like a woman instead of the child you are. You have proved your point well, my love. Around you, I lack control. This never should have happened. From now on, I shall leave you alone. On that, you have my word."

He left the room before I could protest.

I managed to grab the bin beside the cabinet just before I threw up, tears falling with every heave. A vomiting, sobbing mess dressed in expensive green satin. No wonder Kolya hadn't hung around. He regretted being with me. I wasn't what he wanted; he'd made that perfectly clear. I had to think about my future, but I was in no fit state to do that tonight.

I heard the door open and looked up to find Nate walking towards me.

"Hey, Tess, don't cry. It will be all right. I promise," Nate said as he picked me up in his strong arms and carried me to the bathroom. He set me on the edge of the tub and gently wiped my face with a damp washcloth.

"Do you feel as though you need to throw up again?" he asked.

I shook my head—not the best idea under the circumstances. "I'll take the bin to bed with me, just in case," I told him.

"No problem, sweetheart. Let's get you and this pail cleaned up, and then you can settle down and get some sleep. You'll probably be hungover in the morning, so I'll bring you a glass of water and a couple of painkillers."

He helped me stand and then followed me into the bedroom, pulling the quilt back on the bed so I could climb inside.

"Want me to unzip your dress?" he asked.

"Please, if you don't mind."

Nate did as requested and then turned around, giving me privacy while I removed the dress and got into bed.

"I'll lay it over this chair," he said, picking up the crumpled gown.

"Nate, when I said I loved you earlier, I really meant it, you know. It wasn't just the champagne talking."

"I know that, honey. And I love you right back."

"Good. At least someone does," I whispered before drifting off to sleep.

Chapter Twenty

TESS

I woke up early, though I really wish I hadn't. My head was pounding, and my mouth felt dryer than the desert.

Nate had left a glass of water and two paracetamol on the bedside cabinet, God bless him, and I swallowed the pills with slight apprehension. I wasn't sure how well my stomach would react after all the vomiting last night.

No way would I drink champagne again!

I stumbled out of bed and opened a window, letting fresh air into the stuffy room. Although my curls still looked good, my hair felt crusty; I hoped to God it was the hair spray and not dried vomit. A quick, tentative sniff assured me it wasn't the latter.

No matter how *delicate* I felt, I desperately needed a shower. Last night's perfectly made-up face now resembled something from a horror flick, with most of it smeared across the pristine white pillowcases.

I removed the dark, smudged eye makeup and then tied my hair back before stepping under the warm shower spray. I didn't plan on getting my hair wet; I couldn't deal with the effort it would take to control the curls, along with the misery of my first-ever hangover.

Just after I'd finished dressing, there was a knock on my bedroom door. I was about to tell whoever it was to come in, but the words caught in my mouth. What if it was Kolya? What would we say to each other after the events of last night? Was he still angry with me for ruining his schmooze fest with the Frenchman? Would he be full of regret from the fact that we nearly had sex?

I couldn't let him see how hurt I was. I thought after what happened that day at Jean's house when he'd made me experience my first orgasm, that it would bring us closer. But since then, he'd become distant, and it wasn't just the miles apart that created that distance.

I had to face facts: he didn't want me in that way. But I wanted him, more so now than ever before.

Another knock brought me back to the here and now. I quickly scanned the room for my sunglasses, needing to hide my hurt from the man who'd caused it.

"Tess, are you okay in there? I brought you some breakfast." I felt so relieved when I heard it was Nate; I immediately opened the door and ushered him inside.

"Thanks for the breakfast, Nate. And thanks for looking after me last night. I don't know what I'd have done without you."

He'd brought me poached eggs on toast with orange juice and a mug of tea.

"I don't think I can eat anything. I'm still feeling queasy," I admitted.

"You can and you will, Tess, even if it's just one slice of toast and an egg. Trust me, you don't want to get into that helicopter on an empty stomach after the night you had."

The nausea I expected to feel after my first few forkfuls

was surprisingly absent, so I carried on eating, realising this was the first food I'd consumed since yesterday afternoon. We were supposed to eat at the event, but that hadn't gone as planned.

"Where's Kolya?" I asked as I finished drinking my tea.

"He had some business to take care of, but he'll be back soon. We're scheduled to fly in forty-five minutes, so you need to be ready to go by then."

I looked around the room for my sunglasses, trying to remember if I'd worn them yesterday.

"What're you looking for, sweetheart?"

"I can't find my sunglasses. I don't even know if I brought them. My head's all over the place."

"It's overcast today, so I doubt you'll need them," Nate replied reassuringly.

"But I *do* need them, Nate. I can't face Kolya right now without some kind of…" I waved my hand in circles, trying to find the right words to express how I was feeling.

"Protection," he suggested. "Are you trying to hide that you're a little hungover or something else?"

"Both."

"You wanna tell me what that something else is?" he asked.

"No. Because if I do, I know I'll cry, and I did enough of that last night. I doubt my head could take it."

"Okay, so here's what we'll do—we'll throw everything into your suitcase as quick as we can, then go down to the foyer and have ourselves a little retail therapy. The boutique across from the reception desk has Dolce & Gabbana sunglasses that are just waiting for you to buy them. So pick up that little platinum card, and let's go shopping."

"I can't, Nate."

"Why not?"

"It feels wrong to spend Kolya's money when he doesn't know about it."

Three days after Kolya had left on business, I received an envelope addressed to Mrs T Barinov. When I opened it and looked inside, I found a credit card that also had Mrs T Barinov in the bottom left-hand corner. When I'd asked Kolya about it, he said I should use it if I saw anything I liked. He'd already left me one of his cards so I could shop online, but this one was mine. In my new name. I'd stared at it for nearly thirty minutes before I showed Jean and Nan. They told me I had to remember to write my new surname when signing the back. I hadn't used it to buy anything other than the outfit for last night, and that was because Kolya told me I had to buy something suitable. All the treatments I'd had at the spa were charged to Kolya's account. I didn't need to do anything but present myself.

"When you showed me the damn thing yesterday, you didn't say you needed his permission to use it," Nate said.

"I don't need permission. I just... I don't know. I suppose I just feel better if he gives me a reason to use it."

"How about pissing you off last night? Isn't that a reason to use it?"

"I'm not that kind of person, Nate. I wouldn't feel right doing that."

"Then how about we go buy those sunglasses to hide any tears that might fall when you see him? They'll be your armour, Tess—a way to hide how vulnerable you feel. I could tell you a thousand times how wrong you are for not letting him see that you're hurting, but I know you won't listen. Besides, they'll look so damn sexy with your red hair and curls, which is as good a reason as any to make the cash register ring."

Chapter Twenty-One

KOLYA

I stepped into the elevator to find both Franco and Jonesy on either side of Tess. They were whispering something in her ear. At first, she appeared shocked, but then she smiled. The relief I felt eased the tension from my shoulders and upper body. She was happy, or so it seemed.

I'd been worried that the events of last night would have caused her to feel uncomfortable around me. We'd argued like never before, and I almost claimed her innocence with an angry, possessive fuck—something that she and I would have regretted had I done so. Tess was right in everything she'd said.

I have little to no control in her presence.

I was too rough with her last night—I could have hurt her physically and emotionally. Tess would never have forgiven me. So why had I done nothing but relive every second of our ferocious yet passionate encounter?

I chanced a few words with her to see if the happiness she shared with my guards extended my way.

"Are you ready to go home, Tess?"

"Are you?" she replied. Her words were terse, measured, and controlled.

"I am. In future, I will try to limit the time I spend away from home on business," I stated.

"Business. Right," she muttered under her breath.

I had my answer: she had not forgiven me. But out of everything that happened last night, I would not be blamed for something I had not done.

I waited while we were seated in the helicopter before taking her hand in mine.

"Tess, for all the reasons I must apologise to you, being unfaithful is not one of them. I made vows to you before God, and I intend to keep them."

She turned as if to say something in reply, but after a few seconds of hesitation, she turned away.

"What were you going to say, my love?" I questioned. "Tell me, please."

"It doesn't matter, Kolya. Not anymore."

Her eyes were covered by large sunglasses, and her body language—mostly hidden because she faced the window—gave nothing away.

"I have a headache, so if you don't mind, I'd like to close my eyes and try to forget we're flying," she said with a sigh.

"Of course, my love. Champagne can give you a killer hangover, and with everything that happened, we forgot to eat last night. Drinking alcohol on an empty stomach increases the rate of intoxication, and its effects can be felt for some time. When we get home, drink a full glass of water and lie down for a while. Nan has the day off, so Ivan will fire up the barbecue later. After an hour or two of resting, you could join us for something to eat."

She turned to me and smiled, but it wasn't genuine.

"I'll see how I feel after I've slept," was all she said before turning back to the window. I took her hand again and clasped it in my own. She felt cold to the touch. Perhaps she genuinely *was* suffering the effects of last night's champagne, but I had a feeling it was something other than that. Though she sat just a seat away from me in the close confines of the helicopter, the distance between us felt a mile wide.

Chapter Twenty-Two

TESS

I closed my bedroom door and sat on the edge of my bed, contemplating the next few months of my life. It wouldn't be easy leaving Kolya and everyone else behind, but staying here would be more than I could handle. I didn't have any money of my own, but Kolya wouldn't begrudge me the fare to get back to Doncaster. Jean had gone to visit her sister-in-law in Norfolk and wouldn't be home for another five days, but I knew she'd let me stay with her until I could afford to rent my own place.

I heard on the news last week that Hassan Akbar's body had been discovered in the marsh near Fellbrook Woods, near to where they'd found Sarah.

PC Foster had been in touch, asking if I'd seen or heard anything from Hassan since that night outside Jean's house. I told her I hadn't. The police had also launched an investigation into grooming gangs in both Nottingham and Leeds, which PC Foster mentioned was called Operation Midnight. She said she might have more questions for me in the future, and I told her I'd be more than happy to help. Of course, once I'd left Kolya, I wouldn't have his solicitor with me, but I'd learned plenty about lying to the police over the last few weeks, and I'd be lying again when they asked about Hassan Akbar. I knew Kolya had a hand in his death, but he hadn't outright admitted it, and I wasn't about to ask. He'd been visiting his family in Moscow when the police believed Hassan had been murdered.

With Hassan out of the way and Tariq still missing, I felt it was safe for me to go back to Doncaster, but as soon as I could afford it, I would leave that place and all the bad memories it held.

I pulled out one of the suitcases and the overnight bag that Kolya had bought me, wanting to pack as many of my clothes as possible. The ones Kolya purchased when he'd first brought me home didn't fit me anymore. I'd gained weight and gone up two sizes. Good food and Franco's tailored workouts had given me the body of a woman. It was a shame that Kolya didn't see me that way.

I knew leaving was the right thing to do, so why on earth was I crying? I'd barely got half the case packed before I ended up a blubbering mess.

Glancing around the room, I took stock of my possessions, remembering Kolya presenting me with each new gift. My iPad and MacBook, my beloved Kindle. The phone he'd given me when I was in the hospital. I flicked through the photographs I had stored on there and knew I'd treasure them always. There were so many of Nan, Ivan, Danny, Bess, Franco, and Jonesy, though by far the most were of Kolya. I had hundreds of him, but they would never be enough for me. Just looking at them made my heart ache.

His ice-blue eyes were the first thing I ever noticed about him. I swear they hold some sort of magic power. He only has to look at me and raise one brow for my knees to grow weak. When he follows that with his sexy smile, I tingle in all the right places.

I heard shouting and laughing coming from outside, so I put down my phone and went out to investigate. Kolya and a few others had hit the basketball court. I enjoyed watching them play. They were ruthless, often knocking each other over in their mad pursuit of the ball.

I made my way over to the court, passing by Ivan at the barbecue. He handed me a bottle of water from a plastic cooler, along with a plate filled with various cooked meats; the distinct aroma of steaks seared over charcoal made my mouth water.

I watched Kolya take control of the ball and move swiftly around the court. He wore nothing but knee-length shorts and a pair of Nike Air. Sweat glistened over his chest, making the ink on his tattoos appear darker.

When putting my empty plate and bottle on the wall beside me, I noticed Kevin standing next to Ivan. He filled a burger bun with what looked like two steaks and made his way towards me.

"Didn't you fancy joining in?" I asked, nodding towards the men.

"You must be joking. My shoulder's still banged up from the last time I played. Franco's a demon out there, and Jonesy's no better. They are way too competitive for me. Besides, it's nice to just stand here and look, isn't it?"

"Definitely!" I agreed.

All but Danny were shirtless, and every man on that court was a sight to behold, though none more so to me than Kolya. They were all muscle, strength, and hot, sweating maleness. Everyone except Danny was at least six feet in height, though he wasn't far off that number. The sheer power behind their movements, combined with the visual display, made me feel a little warm and flustered. I waved my hand in front of my face to generate cool air.

"I know that feeling," Kevin said with a smirk. We laughed out loud and fist-bumped before continuing our lusty perusal of those fine male specimens.

Nate leapt our way and grabbed the ball before it escaped off the court.

"Like what you see?" he asked.

"You know I do," Kevin replied.

There were a few seconds of silence between them, and it felt as if the air changed, becoming almost stifling. Nate's eyes fixed on Kevin's mouth, and I knew he wanted to kiss him. Instead, with the ball under one arm, he dropped down on one knee and took my hand in his before kissing the back of it. In a dramatic English accent, he asked, "Sweet maiden of the court, will thou wish me luck so I can beat mine opponents?"

I placed my hand on the top of his head and joined in with the fun. "Arise, Sir Nate. Go forth and slay those who darest challenge thee."

There were shouts and jeers from the men on the court, but that changed immediately when Nate ploughed his way through them to take the perfect shot.

"What the…?" Jonesy yelled, before adding, "I'm having some of that."

He ran up to me and kissed me on either cheek before claiming the ball and taking a shot. Again, the ball went straight through the hoop.

"Unfuckingbeliveable," Franco shouted as Jonesy fist-pumped the air.

They carried on playing until Lucas took a tumble, grazing his leg and knee badly. He limped towards a bag on the other end of the court before sticking two fingers up at Dave for heckling him.

I didn't see Franco until he was right in front of me.

"How 'bout you send some of that luck my way, baby?" he said before cupping my cheeks in his hands and dropping his nose to mine. He nuzzled my face before placing a gentle kiss on my forehead. Then he darted towards Kolya, who, as well as dribbling the ball, looked like he wanted to murder him.

Franco took control of the ball and threw it directly through the hoop.

"That was too fuckin' easy, boss. You need to get your head in the game," Franco taunted. Nate laughed and slapped Kolya on the back.

"He had you there, boss. Nothing like a bit of jealousy to throw a man off his game," Jonesy declared.

Kolya glared at me, his face like thunder. I held that glare with one of my own. No way would I let him intimidate me. I hadn't done anything wrong. Well, not in public, anyway. But the thoughts rolling around in my head when Franco's lips were nearing mine…

Kolya's expression changed, but it was no less threatening than before. A predatory smile graced his lips, causing me to swallow nervously. I purposely looked away, watching Lucas hobbling back to the court with a pressure bandage around his knee.

"You're going down, mate," he yelled, gesturing towards Franco.

"Bring it on, pussy," Franco replied.

I looked around for Kolya but realised he'd left the court. I was about to ask Kevin where he'd gone when I was grabbed from behind and then spun around. Kolya's eyes bore into mine, capturing my soul in his heat-filled gaze as he tugged me against him. I should have turned my face away before his lips met mine, but I gave in to him completely. He kissed me with a raw possessiveness that took my breath and left me boneless, caught once again in a web of desire, oblivious to all but him.

A series of whoops and wolf whistles broke through the lust and longing taking over my senses. I pulled away from the kiss and out of Kolya's arms, so angry at both him and myself for the way I'd reacted.

I turned to go without looking at him, but he wasn't having any of it. He grabbed my arm to stop me from fleeing.

"Why, Kolya?" I asked, trying to make sense of what just happened: of why he kissed me like that after what he'd said last night.

"I needed to remind my wife who she belongs to," was all he said before re-joining the game.

"Are you okay?" Kevin placed his hand on my shoulder. "You look a little shell-shocked."

"I'm tired, Kevin, that's all. I think I'll go to my room for a bit. Just make sure none of them break any bones while I'm gone," I said, gesturing towards the court.

He nodded in understanding. "Tess, my door's always open if you ever need to talk."

"Thanks, Kevin. I appreciate that."

My hands shook as I opened the door to my room. Who the hell did Kolya think he was? I belonged to no one. Not after last night. Before that, I would have happily admitted to being his—just like I thought he'd been mine. Looking around at the half-packed suitcases, I knew I'd made the right decision.

It was Nan's day off today. Jack had taken her to the coast, so I didn't want to disturb her, but as soon as I saw her in the morning I'd ask if I could stay at her cottage until Jean came home. It was for the best. Kolya's hot and cold behaviour was messing with my head.

With my mind made up, I went into the en-suite and ran a bath, pouring in the lavender-scented bath and shower gel Jean had bought me. It said on the label it was supposed to *"calm the senses,"* so I added an extra capful for good measure. God knows I needed it.

After undressing, I lowered myself into the warm, bubble-filled water, resting my head against the back of the tub. I'm not sure if it was the lavender or the heat from the water seeping into my skin, but after a few minutes, I began to relax. Until I thought of that kiss again, along with the one from last night. How is it possible that a man can make you cry and then turn you on just hours later?

Every kiss I've had from Kolya has given me an intense reaction *down there*. Even though he hadn't touched me in that way, he'd already given me an orgasm. I'd tried to do it myself since, but it never felt right. Even as I slipped my hand below the water to find the right spot, it didn't feel as good as when Kolya pressed against me. Maybe you just can't do it in the bath.

Girls at school never talked about doing it themselves. They talked about their boyfriends and what they did with them, and I think there was a lot of exaggeration going on when they bragged about how good it was.

I didn't have anyone I could really talk to about sex. I couldn't imagine ever having that kind of conversation with Nan or Jean, and I was no longer in touch with any of the friends I'd hung around with at school. I knew where my clitoris was situated. I'd studied the leaflet that came with every box of tampons, and I'd read enough saucy romance novels to know I was supposed to have a G-spot somewhere inside.

When the water began to cool, I reached for the towel and climbed out. After brushing my teeth, I put on my nightie and climbed into bed. I needed to close the drawers I'd left open and zip up the suitcase, but I didn't have the heart. Doing so would bring me closer to leaving, and though I knew it was for the best, it still hurt to think about it.

After what Kolya said to me when he kissed me earlier, I was more confused than ever. Obviously, other than Kolya, I have no experience with the opposite sex, but the way he looked at me after he'd kissed me—when he was reminding me I was his—it felt like he really meant it.

Remembering how passionately he'd kissed me made my sex throb once again. With my hands already under the quilt, I tugged up my nightie and began a slow exploration. This time, my fingers hit the right spot almost immediately. I rocked my hips in time with the movement of my hand and closed my eyes, letting myself succumb to each new sensation. I dipped a finger inside me and used some of the wetness I found to rub over my sensitive little nub, and eventually, with a little more pressure and friction, I could feel an orgasm building. A soft moan and then a gasp escaped my mouth, but just as I was about to come, there was a knock on my bedroom door.

"Tess, are you all right?" Kolya asked as he strode into my room. He spotted my suitcase and the open drawers and froze.

"Are you going somewhere, my love?" He was still shirtless and wore the same grey shorts.

I brought my hands out from under the quilt and pulled it up under my chin. I could feel the heat from the blush on my cheeks. He'd nearly caught me touching myself.

"I thought I'd ask Nan if I could stay with her until Jean gets back from her holiday," I told him.

"I see," he said, his voice quiet. "Can I ask why?"

"I think it's the right thing to do, for both of us, Kolya."

"I disagree, Tess. A wife belongs with her husband."

"What if that husband doesn't want to be with his wife? If he touches her and then regrets it. What should she do then?" I cried.

He sat on the bed and took my hands in his. I tried to pull them away, but he held them tight.

"I made a vow, Tess. I said I would not make love to you until you were ready. You are only weeks away from turning eighteen. We have to wait. It is the right thing to do."

"For whom, Kolya? This seems to be all about you and what you feel is right. What about me and my feelings?"

"Please, Tess, don't make this more difficult than it already is." Kolya brought my hands to his face and kissed my fingers. In a matter of seconds, his eyes widened, and his nostrils flared. He knew what I'd been up to when he'd walked in. I thought he might stop what he was doing, but he didn't. After kissing each finger, he sucked them into his mouth, groaning when the taste of me hit his tongue.

"Did you think of me?" he murmured.

"Yes," I admitted breathlessly, my embarrassment replaced by nervous excitement.

Kolya let go of my hands and grabbed the quilt. He closed his eyes for a moment, his brows furrowed and his body tense. Kolya seemed at war with himself—like he was struggling to come to terms with something. A strange sound tore from his parted lips. At first, it sounded like the whine of a wounded animal, but then it changed, becoming a deep and guttural growl. When his eyes opened, I knew the fight was over.

My eyes never moved from his as he tugged the quilt down below my knees. My nightie was still bunched up around my waist, leaving me exposed to him, but he didn't look down. I felt his hands moving slowly up the insides of my thighs, and my breath caught in my throat. Only when his thumbs brushed over the wetness at my core did his eyes travel lower.

The embarrassment I thought I'd feel when he saw my naked lower half was strangely absent. Instead, I felt emboldened by his obvious appreciation.

Kolya leaned down and pressed his lips against my sex, gently at first, then the pressure increased when his tongue breached my folds. I let out a breathless gasp as he thrust his tongue inside me, then he slowly traced the tip from my opening to the sensitive little bud hidden below my cleft. He pulled back slightly to place kisses around my lower lips and the inside of my thighs before his tongue retraced the path his lips had travelled. He used his thumbs to open me up to him before sucking gently on every exposed part of me.

There's really no word for the high-pitched noise I made when he fluttered his tongue rapidly over my swollen clit. It was ecstasy. So many feelings came crashing over me at once, resulting in both anxiousness and panic, and then an overriding need to come. I ran my hands through Kolya's hair, unsure whether I wanted to pull him closer or push him away. When he gently slipped a finger inside me, it took the choice right out of my hands. The orgasm hit me hard and sent me soaring. My body seized with involuntary spasms, my back arching without any effort. I cried out his name over and over, moaning and panting as his tongue and lips continued their pleasurable assault. I came again, my body readily accepting the second finger he slipped inside me.

I lay there in utter bliss as he brought me down from the orgasmic high.

"That was amazing," I told him. "But I want more, Kolya. I need to know what it feels like to have all of you."

He gazed up at me; his wide shoulders between my thighs, his short, neat beard glistening wet, wearing my pleasure like he owned it. Kolya's eyes were hooded and full of the promise of more, making me sigh with relief. He wasn't going to stop. Not this time.

Pressing tender kisses to my lower belly—followed by soft, wet licks—he made his way up my body, pausing for a moment to rid me of my nightdress. When he arrived at my breasts, he cupped them gently, rolling my nipples with his thumbs and forefingers. My nipples hardened under his expert touch, and I moaned deeply when he increased the pressure. Just as his touch became almost painful, he replaced his hands with his mouth, causing a flood of heat and arousal to pool in my sex.

Though I'd never made love before, I knew my body was ready for him. I didn't expect to feel any pain; I'd been using tampons for a while, so I knew there'd be no barrier to stop him. Even if there was pain, I'd willingly take it.

He pulled away from me slightly, making me think he'd changed his mind. When his hands went to the waistband of his shorts, I sighed with relief. The sigh turned into an anxious gasp when I saw Kolya's thick, heavy length. I licked my lips nervously. Those previous feelings of want and need changed to *"What the fuck was I thinking?"*

"Touch me, Tess. I've waited so long for your caress."

The raw hunger in his voice elicited a different reaction than the one I'd had only seconds before. I knew at that moment that he craved the joining of our bodies as much as I did, and although he'd had years of sexual experience, for him, making love to me for the first time would mean so much more. I felt more confident—as if there'd been a sudden shift in the balance of power. Yes, Kolya owned my pleasure tonight, but I owned his, too.

I wrapped my right hand around his length, wondering how hard to grip him. His cock felt...good. Hot and hard, yet the skin surrounding it was soft to the touch. I ran my hand over him gently. He was slightly veiny in places, yet the head was so smooth, and there was a sticky, clear fluid leaking from the tip. Kolya threw his head back and groaned. He looked like a work of art that you'd pay to see. Every muscle in his perfect body had tensed, his facial expression a strange mix of both pleasure and pain.

I'd caused that. I made this beautiful, strong man throb in my hand.

The fear I'd had at the size of him quickly fled. When he opened his eyes and looked down at me, I nodded, expressing my consent. It was time.

Kolya rested his left forearm by the side of my head as he kissed me. I could smell and taste my essence on his lips, but it didn't bother me. He placed his right hand over my own and began rubbing his length over my sex, lubricating it with the slickness he'd created. Even though I wanted this more than anything, I still tensed when I felt the blunt head of his erection at my opening.

Kolya let go of his cock and placed his finger over my clit. It didn't take long for him to have me moaning softly, undulating my hips to take him deeper inside me. He removed his fingers and spoke in hurried, whispered Russian before looking into my eyes and saying, "Forgive me, Tess." Then he thrust his hips forward, burying his thick, hard length deep inside me.

I cried out from the shock and discomfort of the sudden invasion. It wasn't exactly painful; I just felt uncomfortably over-stretched. He swore in both English and Russian before resting his forehead against my own, exhaling a long, deep breath.

"I will treasure this gift you have given me, Tess. I will hold it in my heart along with your first declaration of love."

I put my arms around his shoulders and held his loving gaze. "Everything we do will be a first for me, Kolya. Is your heart big enough to hold it all?"

"My darling, before you, my heart was an unfeeling, broken mess. Only my son caused it to beat. Now it beats for you, too, and it's stronger than ever. You have mended what was broken, Tess. No words of gratitude are adequate for all you have done for me."

"Then show me, Kolya. Now. Like this. Show me with your body how much I mean to you."

He withdrew almost all the way, then pushed back in slowly. I can't say it was pleasurable; it just felt…wrong. Unnatural, even. I had something huge inside me that felt too big to be there. It wasn't until his lips met mine in an all-consuming kiss that the feel of him changed. His kiss took over my thoughts and feelings, his lips never leaving mine for even a second as his tongue mimicked the actions happening below. It was as much an assault on my senses as it was on my lips.

The change, when it happened, wasn't a gradual thing. It was as though someone had switched on the pleasure button, and what had previously felt wrong now felt *Oh. So. Right!*

My hips tilted towards him of their own accord, and a flood of arousal eased his way. Kolya trailed kisses over my jaw and throat, pausing at my collarbone to suck on the skin. When he came to the scar below it, he placed gentle kisses over and around it, whispering in Russian once again.

His lips trailed even lower, yet he was still moving inside me. I cried out his name when he suckled on and around my sensitive nipples. Everything felt so good—like my breasts had a direct line to my clit, causing it to swell and throb as he rocked against me. I pushed up against him, needing to feel more of…this…of us, and the intense feeling building inside me. Kolya kissed his way back to my mouth and held me as the orgasm raced through my body. His thrusts became harder and somehow deeper until he threw his head back and groaned, his cock pulsing inside me as he came.

Chapter Twenty-Three

TESS

I woke up alone, much to my dismay. Kolya had a meeting in London this morning, so he'd had to leave early. I must have been dead to the world when he'd left my bed; I'd not even heard the helicopter take off. But then again, Kolya and I had been pretty active last night.

After he'd made love to me the first time, he suggested we shower. He'd come straight to my room after playing basketball yesterday, and sex appears to be quite a messy act where sheets are concerned. We'd got each other clean in between soft, slow kisses, but that changed when Kolya pressed me up against the cold tile and devoured my lips like a man possessed. He teased my sex again with his skilled fingers and showed me how he liked to be touched. I wasn't sure I was doing it right at first; I didn't feel confident in gripping him as firmly as he'd told me. But then he flexed his hips, causing me to stroke him faster, and I watched in pure fascination when he came on my belly. When his breathing had slowed a little, Kolya dropped to his knees and made me come with his tongue once again. I suppose I should have offered to return the favour, but I was a little anxious about it, if I'm honest. He's not a small man down there, and I was sure I'd gag and mess it up. Kolya never even suggested it, though he'd been more than generous with me on that front.

When we came back to bed, we talked well into the night. He told me how he'd been feeling about being with me sexually. How he'd wanted me to be ready so that I'd not regret giving him my virginity. I was annoyed that he thought me too young to make that kind of decision, but I also felt relieved that I'd not been pressured into having sex —like Sarah and some of the other girls at school. Kolya respected me enough to wait, even though he wanted me so desperately.

I also spoke to him about contraception and the fact we'd had unprotected sex. He said he'd always worn a condom whenever he'd been with a woman—something he hadn't done since he met me. I told him I was about mid-cycle, so we'd taken a big risk by not using anything. He looked me in the eye and said he didn't regret anything about our lovemaking, and if I were to become pregnant with his child, he would be the happiest man alive. I didn't know what to say to that. I knew I wanted children some-day, but I'd just left school without finishing my A levels and hadn't even had a job. I told him if I ended up preg-nant at eighteen years old, I would be like the typical stereotype of someone from my background. Kolya dismissed this with a laugh before saying, "So a pregnant teenager with your background is usually married to a billionaire and is chauffeured around in a luxury car or flies in a helicopter to avoid traffic. And I suppose they would all have an unlimited budget with which to purchase designer maternity clothing and baby items, along with the very best in private antenatal care during their pregnancy."

When he put it like that, I could see how different it would be, but I still couldn't imagine myself as a mum. Not yet, anyway.

Kolya noticed how quiet I'd gone and turned to face me. He kissed my lips lightly and gazed down at me, saying, "Tess, I'm forty-one. I know men are supposed to produce active sperm their entire life, but I know of quite a few men my age who've had problems conceiving a child. If you want to have a family with me, we should think about doing it within the next couple of years. I don't want to be an old father of a young child. I want to be fit and active enough to play football with them, and not show up at a school event looking like their grandfather."

For the first time, I could see our relationship from Kolya's point of view. I always looked to him to be the strong one who would guide me through my insecurities, but I wasn't the only one feeling insecure. I hated to think that Kolya felt anything other than complete happiness about our relationship. So I made a decision, right there and then, declaring, "I think we should forget about contraception, Kolya. Like you said, I won't have the same financial worries as other young mums, and we *are* married. Besides, I might not get pregnant for ages yet. I mean, you hear of couples trying for a baby for years and—"

Before I could finish speaking, Kolya had taken over my mouth with a passionate, toe-curling kiss—one that made me instantly wet and ready for him. He ground his sex against my own and had me moaning and chanting his name over and over. Just as I began to come, he pushed inside me and made love to me slowly, telling me how much he loved and adored me with every thrust; how he would always be there for me whenever I needed him, and what my words had meant to him. We climaxed together, showering each other with kisses and further declarations of love and hope for our future.

It seems strange to say that a sexual act was beautiful, but that's what it was to me. Beautiful and meaningful, and falling asleep in my husband's arms after we'd shared so much intimacy was the icing on the cake. But that was last night. Now I had to get up and face everyone. They must have known what we'd been doing because it was still quite early when Kolya came to my room. Most of the men would have gone to the older part of the house, but Nate and Kevin lived in the extension with us. What if they'd heard us? I hadn't been quiet when I'd been in the throes of orgasm. It had happened so many times, too. I debated staying in my room all day, so I wouldn't have to face them, but I was hungry and needed at least two cups of tea to start the day. So, after taking a shower and dressing, I walked into the kitchen to face the music.

Nan was busy sorting through the cupboards. She turned my way and smiled. "Good morning, Tess. The kettle's just boiled. I'll have a cuppa if you're making one."

I grabbed two cups from the cupboard and proceeded to make our tea.

"There you go," I said while handing her a cup. "What are you looking for, Nan?"

"The deep pie dish. The one I make the apple and pear cinnamon sponge in. I was going to make one for later, but I just can't find it."

"Did you check the men's kitchen? Franco and Ivan love anything with cinnamon."

"I haven't. Though I don't know why. If anything goes

missing, it's usually over there. Do you fancy going with me to retrieve it once you've had your breakfast?"

"Umm, no, I'd better not," I replied. I could feel the heat of the blush colouring my cheeks.

"Tess, is there a reason why you don't want to go?" she asked.

"I can't face them. Not today, anyway."

"Can't face who? Ivan and Franco?"

"All of them, Nan. Not after last night."

"Why? What happened last night?" she asked. She seemed an equal mix of concerned and confused.

"Last night, Kolya and I, *you know*, for the first time. I'm not sure if any of them came into this part of the house. Nate and Kevin live here, so they probably know. I'll be so embarrassed if they say anything, or if they just look at me, even."

Nan smiled and placed her hand on my arm. "Tess, you and Kolya are married. What you do behind closed doors shouldn't concern anyone else—as long as things are consensual. I've known Kolya for a long time. He's a good man, and someone I trust will take care of you. But if there's anything you need to talk about, no matter how embarrassing or inappropriate, you can always tell me. I might not have all the answers, but I promise to help if I can."

"We didn't use protection," I admitted. "I know Kolya will take care of me, but what if I end up pregnant? I don't know the first thing about babies. I know I want one someday, but I don't know if I'm ready for that yet. What if I'm totally crap at being a mum? My own mum was terrible. It was me who looked after her. My grandma is a royal bitch and probably holds the title of *The World's Shittiest Mother and Grandmother.* What if the apple doesn't fall far from the tree?

What if I'm incapable of being a good mum due to genetics?"

Nan shook her head. "Like you said, you took care of your mum. You loved her even though she wasn't a good mother to you. You have it in you to care for someone and to love them unconditionally. And I will be here to help you every step of the way, along with Kolya and the rest of his staff. Everyone will love and spoil your children, Tess. You don't need to worry about that. But I understand you are young and probably need time to adjust to being an adult before you bring a child into the world. Did you discuss this with Kolya?"

"I was going to, but then he said he didn't want to be an older dad who looked like his child's grandad, and I think he was worried about his fertility, too. I get where he's coming from, Nan, I really do. I just... I don't know. Maybe I should talk to him about it again. I said we didn't have to use anything, but now I'm just not sure."

"Tess, if it's not the right time for you, we can go to the pharmacy and get you the morning-after pill. Kolya is your husband, not your keeper. He shouldn't have any say over your body." She said this in all seriousness. Knowing she had my back, whatever my decision, almost made me cry.

"No, Nan, it's fine. I'll be okay. I'd rather talk to Kolya about it first. Thanks for offering to help, though. I really appreciate it."

"Tess, you are like family to me. The daughter I never had. I'll always be here for you no matter what happens in your life," she declared with a reassuring smile. "Now, are we going to get my pie dish while I'm still in a baking mood?"

"I don't know. Do you think they'll be able to tell if they see me? Do I look different, Nan?"

"You look happier, Tess. And even though you have something on your mind, you seem a lot less troubled. But then you always are whenever Kolya's home. Do you feel any different?" she asked.

Did I feel different? I suppose I did, really. I definitely felt more relaxed. And I also felt like I belonged here now. In Kolya's home. Our home. The home in which we would raise our children. Together. I now had specific roles that entitled me to be here: wife, lover, and eventually, mother.

I looked at Nan and smiled. "Yes, I do feel different. More settled, I suppose."

With my hand on my lower belly, I wondered what the future might hold. Had Kolya and I conceived already?

Chapter Twenty-Four

KOLYA

After several hours in the office, I realised my workday was fucked. Despite having important issues to deal with, my time here hadn't proved productive. Thoughts of Tess filled my head, taking over completely.

I shouldn't have come in today, no matter how important my meetings were.

I needed to be at home with my wife. Preferably in bed, enjoying the pleasures only she could give. Pleasures I had denied myself for so long.

I looked over the plans on my desk once again, trying to be more critical of our latest design. My engineering team and I did this several times before final approval, but today, I found myself unable to criticise anything on the drawings in front of me. I pulled up the 3D image on the monitor and studied it closely.

The SAM—surface-to-air missile—launcher will tick many boxes for our buyers. It's smaller and lighter than our other anti-aircraft designs, meaning it's easily transportable, and we've created new technology that will send the missiles it carries further than any other SAM on the market.

Our first anti-aircraft weapon propelled KOLCAT into the big league as far as weapons providers were concerned, but my team and I know that this particular missile launcher—WREX.24065, or Rex, as the designers like to call it—will be a game changer in the world of modern warfare. The new computerised targeting methods, combined with our advanced engineering, make it currently second to none.

This was the first time since brainstorming our ideas that technical drawings of the launcher had been presented. My team from KOLCAT UK travelled down to London from Northampton to discuss where we were at with the design and brought the first drafts along for me to study. We should have the prototype ready for testing within a year. With the sophistication of today's technology, it's now much quicker to bring our ideas to fruition than when KOLCAT was in its infancy.

Work had always been a priority for me. I'm ashamed to say that my focus had been on building my company in my younger years, instead of building my family. When I lost Catherine, that had to change, and it did for a while until James went to study in the States. Don't get me wrong, I still worked most days, but I made sure I was there for my boy as much as I could be. Nan was a godsend, and I wouldn't have coped in that first year without her and Jack. I don't think I could have carried on without her presence and support.

Although KOLCAT is still very important to me, I am determined not to let it take over my life this time around. Tess and any children we have will be my priority going forward. James is at an age where he doesn't need his father as much. It happens to us all and was something I felt keenly when I first noticed it.

A month after he'd moved to the States, our phone and video calls became less frequent. College and new friends replaced father-and-son time. Women speak openly about empty-nest syndrome, but it affects men, too. Nan and I suffered from it for weeks after James left. To help her cope, Nan joined a nearby yoga class and took on extra work as a seamstress—not because she needed the money, she just needed something to fill up her time. I worked like crazy and hit the gym when I came home, hanging out with my guards where possible. The things we did helped, but the loneliness and empty feelings were still there.

Neither of us has felt that way since Tess came into our lives.

My thoughts drifted away from the 3D image in front of me, and once again, I pictured Tess in my mind's eye.

I'd watched her sleep for thirty minutes this morning. Wayward curls had covered her pillow and shoulders. Tess had slept on her front, her face turned to the side. She looked so serene. I've watched her sleep many times over the past few months, but this morning was the first time I'd seen her look peaceful since hearing about Sarah's death.

I placed my hand on her lower back, just above the rounded cheeks of her shapely bottom. The weight and muscle tone she'd gained after coming to live with me gave her curves I'd often fantasised about touching and kissing. She was exquisite, and she was all mine. I kissed the many freckles on her shoulder before whispering I love you, then I left her room so I wouldn't wake her when I took a shower. I was hard enough to hammer nails, but I didn't take myself in hand like I had so many times since meeting her. It seemed wrong to relieve myself of something that belonged to her now.

It felt good to belong to someone again. More than good, actually. It felt…right. Like my world was finally as it should be.

When I walked into her room and saw her half-packed suitcase, I felt chilled to the bone. She'd been ready to leave me, and it had been my fault. By trying to do the right thing, I'd made her feel unwanted. Undesired. That couldn't have been further from the truth.

When I smelled and then tasted her essence on her fingers, I knew I'd not be leaving her bed without having more.

She'd thought of me when she touched herself. It made the erection I'd had since I'd kissed her fingers even harder. She told me she wanted all of me. She already had my heart and soul; the only thing I'd not given her was my body. With the taste of her still on my tongue, I let go of those misguided scruples that had almost made her leave and buried myself inside my untouched wife, claiming her virginity in the most exhilarating act of lovemaking I have ever experienced.

Everything about last night was perfect. But then again, my wife is perfect, so how could it have been anything less?

Seeing Tess completely naked for the first time both thrilled and settled me. Undressed, she was all woman. Her pert breasts filled my large hands with a little to spare. Tawny pink nipples stood proud from slightly paler areolae, and a neat triangle of copper-coloured pubic hair covered her sex. She looked like a goddess, so I worshipped her with everything I had.

I couldn't wait to do it all again.

I took out my phone and scrolled through the live camera feeds at home, needing to know what Tess was doing. She was in the kitchen with Nan peeling apples and pears. I longed to erase the distance between us, but I had set up a video conference call with my team in the States, and James will sit in on the meeting. I enjoy seeing him become more involved in KOLCAT. He has fresh ideas and already displays sound leadership skills.

I am immensely proud of my son and the man he is becoming. I don't want to wish the years away, yet I cannot wait to see him take over KOLCAT in America. James is a born leader; KOLCAT will thrive in his hands.

I closed the camera feed and was about to put my phone away when it rang.

"Hello, Yannis. How are you on this fine day?"

"Ready for the break, my friend. I'll be arriving in London tomorrow evening. Will you be at the hotel or home in Oxford?"

"I will be at home tomorrow. I'm finding it hard to be away from my wife, so I'll work from home for the next couple of weeks."

I had forgotten about Yannis's plans to visit. While I couldn't wait for Tess to meet him, I wanted to spend some quality time alone with her.

"You should take her on a spectacular honeymoon, Kolya. I'm sure whatever you have going on at work can wait." Yannis's tone was reprimanding, a complete change from what it was two weeks ago regarding Tess.

"I have something planned that will coincide with Tess's birthday. I want to give her a honeymoon she will never forget," I told him.

"How did your meeting go with Monsieur Alleman?" Yannis

asked. I sighed heavily, then told him about Tess threatening Caroline Dawson and the fact that Alleman had avoided me since.

Yannis laughed loudly before saying, *"I wish I could have been there, Kolya. You know how much I loathe Caroline Dawson. I think Tess and I will become great friends."* Yannis laughed again before adding, *"Will you and Tess be attending this year's hoteliers' ball in Paris? Perhaps they could invite Caroline and sell ringside seats."*

"Very funny, Yannis." He was starting to annoy me and must have heard it in my voice.

"Relax, Kolya. I know the evening didn't bring the outcome you wanted, but think about it. Your wife was willing to fight for you in front of a room full of important people. You have someone who values your marriage more than the need to impress anyone. That kind of woman is not so easy to find, my friend."

He was right, of course. On the evening itself, I'd been shocked and angry at Tess's behaviour, but the scornful looks she'd received as we left angered me more. How dare anyone look at my wife with anything other than respect? Monsieur Alleman could fuck off as far as I was concerned.

There were others within the EU's political hierarchy who could further my cause. Some might think my endeavours with them were an unnecessary headache. After all, I had billions in the bank and could afford to do this without them. But when you are looking at a fifty million turnover on a new site within the first four years, the less tax you pay on that, the better.

"I am a lucky man, Yannis."

"Indeed, you are. And I will finally get to meet your beautiful wife in person tomorrow evening."

I heard the unmistakable sound of aircraft engines before Yannis told me he was about to board his plane. I wished him a safe journey and told him I would get Ivan to fly him from London to Oxford.

I would have loved for Ivan to fly me back to Oxford immediately, but when I hung up on Yannis, my PA told me it was time for my conference call.

Chapter Twenty-Five

TESS

It was 9 p.m. by the time I heard the helicopter's rotor blades signalling Kolya's arrival. I'd spoken to him earlier and knew he expected to be home around 6 p.m. at the latest, but something had come up at KOLCAT's German site, so he'd had to sort out whatever that was before he came home. I was sorry that he'd had to work so late, but in a way, I'd been glad of it, too. I needed to get a few things straight in my head before he came home—my feelings about pregnancy and contraception were at the top of that list.

I didn't mention it on the phone, and honestly, I wondered if it was worth all the worry. I also thought it was embarrassing to talk about. We had to take sex education classes at school, and there'd been so much giggling and heckling coming from both the girls and boys in my class, I'd barely heard what the teacher had to say. They gave us booklets and handouts to look at, but most had been used before, and someone had drawn a huge, hairy-balled penis on the one I had.

I'd seen condoms before. Mum used to get them free from some junkie support group she went to. She'd often take me with her when we couldn't pay the heating bills. It was warm there, and you could get free tea, coffee, and hot chocolate, along with chocolate chip cookies and fruit. They shut the group down due to lack of funding, so Mum's free condom source went too. I once overheard her talking to Paula, one of her addict friends, who was also on the game. Mum said some men would pay ten quid extra to have sex without protection. As far as I'm aware, she never caught anything, and thankfully, she didn't end up pregnant. She wouldn't have been able to stay clean even if she had.

Thinking about how Mum made her living made me cringe. To think that men paid her to do that and more seemed so far removed from what Kolya and I did last night. She'd bring home random strangers: men of all ages, shapes, and sizes. Most looked clean, but occasionally she'd have one that looked positively filthy. She didn't discriminate if it meant losing out on her next fix.

I could hear someone talking outside, so I put the kettle on to make Kolya a cup of tea. I had one of the new minty hot chocolates that Nan had bought and sat on one of the high stools at the breakfast bar. My hair was still slightly damp on the ends after my shower, and I wore a midnight-blue satin nightdress and robe that Kolya had bought for me. I was trying to look sexy for him, I suppose, but the white fluffy bunny slippers probably spoiled the look.

I was grateful there was just me in the kitchen. None of the guys had said anything about Kolya and me today. Jonesy, Lucas, Ivan, and Nate had been in London with Kolya, but I'd seen most of the others, and they hadn't even raised their eyebrows when they saw me. I forget sometimes that I'm dealing with adults now. They aren't anything like the lads at school or at The Willows, though they all like to joke around, especially Ivan and Jonesy.

Franco seemed a lot grumpier than usual. After I'd helped Nan with her baking, he came to find me and suggested we go to the shooting range. He looked every inch the brooding Italian, and I wondered what had pissed him off.

The range had felt cooler today. I'd worn my new in-ear ear defenders and safety glasses, which fitted much better than the others I'd been using. Franco handed me a Glock 17 9mm Luger, though I prefer to use a rifle. I have much better accuracy with my Ruger than any handgun I've tried.

I can never keep my hands steady when holding a pistol. They make it look so easy on TV, but it's not. Once you load the magazine, it feels heavier than it looks, and the recoil makes my hands feel weird. I don't think I'll ever be able to shoot one-handed.

Franco let me practise by loading just five bullets, which made the gun feel a lot lighter. He said the standard version held between fifteen and seventeen rounds, but this gun could hold thirty.

After a few minutes, I added fifteen bullets and tried again. With my arms stretched out in front of me, I took aim at the dark silhouette figure but missed the target completely. Franco shook his head and came to stand close behind me. He placed his arms and hands over mine, holding them steady. He used his knee to nudge my legs open and told me to hold my position for five seconds before firing.

After hitting the outside of the target with the first two shots, my aim went wide, and I lowered my arms in frustration.

"I can't get it right," I complained. "It feels awkward; too heavy in my hands, and it's making my arms ache."

"You need to concentrate more, focus on the target. Centre yourself. Here, let's try this," he said as he placed his hands below my belly button. "Take your strength from here, deep in your belly. Let it rise up through your arms as you aim. Let your core muscles take the strain." I felt his lips brush my ear as he added, "Now imagine we loaded this gun with horse shit instead of bullets, and that target is Caroline Dawson."

I pictured her smug face and proceeded to shoot, firing off twelve shots in one go. Franco took his hands from my belly and pressed the button to reel the target in. I'd delivered five shots to the chest and seven to the mouth.

"Great job, Tess! You certainly made her eat shit. Feel like having another go?"

We did three more timed rounds, and each shot hit the target. By the third round, my arms started shaking again, so Franco called it quits. He was quiet when we cleaned the guns and put everything away, so I asked if he was okay. He looked up at me and stared for a few seconds before he spoke.

"You know I'm here for you, right? If you need anything at all, you only gotta ask, and it's yours."

"Right back at you, Franco," I told him. I wondered if he'd overheard my conversation with Nan earlier. I hoped not.

He stepped towards me and placed his hands on my cheeks. Looking into my eyes, he said, "You can count on me, Tess. I'll always protect you. But I need to go home for a while so I can get my head around…stuff." He let go of me and took a step back. "I'm flying home tomorrow to stay with my sister and her family. You can call or message me anytime."

I nodded slowly, unable to say anything at that moment. It wasn't so much his words that had rendered me speechless; they were just sentences to reassure and provide information. It was the feeling that so much had been left unsaid that made me swallow hard and breathe a little deeper. The surrounding air was thick with tension, and I wasn't the only one affected. Franco's handsome face seemed paler and was devoid of its usual confident expression. He looked... vulnerable. His dark chocolate eyes were filled with sadness, and I worried that something was dreadfully wrong.

"What is it, Franco? What aren't you telling me? Is your sister okay? Is she ill? Is that why you're going to stay with her?"

I threw my arms around him and hugged him tightly. "The calls and messages work both ways, remember? If you need me, Franco, I'm all yours."

"I'd like that, baby, more than you know," he'd whispered before pressing his face into my neck and breathing deeply.

That worrying conversation was still on my mind, so I decided to ask Nate and Jonesy if they knew whether his sister and her family were okay.

Ivan was the first to enter the kitchen. He headed straight for the covered pie dish, picked it up, kissed my cheek, and then asked if we had any custard. Before I could answer, I heard Kolya ask, "Could you give us a little privacy, gentlemen?"

I turned around to find Kolya staring at me. Jonesy and Nate were behind him.

"Sure thing, boss," Nate said before grabbing an apple

from the fruit bowl as Ivan grunted something in Russian. They all wished me goodnight, then left Kolya and me alone.

He took out his phone and pressed a few buttons, switching off the in-house cameras and remotely locking the door.

"I hope you don't watch me through those," I told him, looking at each of the cameras. He said nothing, just raised one eyebrow and continued staring.

"I think it's creepy," I stated.

"I like to see you," he replied. "It calms me."

Kolya's eyes never moved from mine, his expression undeterminable. He was making me nervous.

"Is something wrong, Kolya?" I asked, a slight quiver in my voice.

"The whole day has been wrong, Tess. I should have been here with you. It wasn't enough just to hear your voice and see you on a screen. I should have been able to touch you, kiss you, and make love to you."

"Well, you're here with me now."

Kolya nodded, still holding my gaze.

"How are you feeling?" he asked. His eyes left mine for the first time since he'd entered the kitchen, glancing down towards my lady parts as he spoke.

I felt the blush hit my cheeks as I replied, "I was sore this morning, but I'm okay now."

"That's good to hear, my love," he said as he pushed my legs apart and stepped between my knees. He slipped his hands beneath the hem of my knee-length nightdress, tracing his fingers up the inside of my thighs. When he reached my knickers, he gently ran his fingers over my lace-covered sex.

"When I remove these, will I find you wet for me?" he asked in a voice that was pure sin.

"You know you will," I told him breathlessly.

He began tugging on my knickers, so I placed my hand over his.

"Not here, Kolya. Nate or Kevin could walk in."

"I can assure you they won't."

"We should go to bed," I told him.

"No. When I watched you today, you were over there, peeling fruit. So domesticated. I imagined you lying on the countertop with your legs spread wide, ready for me to eat my fill. Would you like that, Tess?" he whispered before running his tongue over my right ear.

I tried to say yes, but it came out as a whimper, so I nodded instead. Kolya took off his suit jacket and tie, discarding them on the floor beside us, then he hitched my nightdress up and asked me to lift my bottom off the stool so he could remove my knickers. Even though he'd assured me that Nate and Kevin wouldn't disturb us, I still glanced towards the door that led to the hallway and their rooms.

"I need you," Kolya whispered, before lifting me up onto the breakfast bar. He pressed his hand to my chest, pushing me down so I lay flat against the cool marble, then he hooked my legs over his shoulders and used his mouth to make me forget about anything but him and what he was doing to me. I kept my breathy moans as quiet as I could, but as soon as my body climbed that glorious peak, they became much harder to hide.

When my orgasm waned, Kolya lifted me up and placed me back on the barstool. In between sensual, tongue-filled kisses, I heard the jangle of a belt buckle, followed by the lowering of a zipper.

He groaned my name as he entered my body. The

reverence in his voice wasn't lost on me, despite the way he thrust so forcefully. I held on to his shoulders as he pulled me onto his hot length, both of us trying to keep up with frantic kisses in between cries of pleasure and words of love. The stool scraped loudly against the floor when he picked up the pace, but I didn't care who heard us at that point; the look on Kolya's face when we both found heaven cocooned me from thoughts of anyone but us.

Chapter Twenty-Six

TESS

Yannis Markos is smart, funny, loves animals, and can't stand Caroline *Bitchface* Dawson, so we get along brilliantly. He's been staying with us for the past week and has invited us to go back to Greece with him to stay on his island.

Fancy being so rich that you own an island!

Because Yannis isn't married and doesn't have any kids of his own, he's arranged for Kolya's son to inherit the island and everything he owns. As if James isn't wealthy enough already! The saying *"money goes to money"* is most certainly true.

It's such a shame he doesn't have someone to share his life with. His father and his first wife betrayed him in the worst possible way, and his last two wives were just after his money, it seems. But there's so much more to Yannis, and he's drop dead gorgeous in that sexy Mediterranean way.

Standing at around five foot ten with an athletic build, light brown eyes, and coal-black hair, Yannis will have plenty of women after him wherever he goes. Yet he says he's not interested in getting married again. I find that quite sad.

Kolya and I are so happy together—now that he's no longer worried about my age. Our days are filled with happy smiles, holding hands, kisses, and love; our nights are dominated by unrestrained passion and sexual need. I can't get enough of him and never dreamed it was possible to be so happy.

Watching the banter between Kolya and Yannis as they sat talking about their time at university made me smile. I'm surprised they passed any of their exams. It reminded me of the messages Franco and I had been sending each other for the past few days. His family is doing well, and he's enjoyed spending time with them, especially his nephew and niece. In our messages, he's been telling me to carry on with my education. I'd studied for two years for my A levels but missed all my exams because I was hiding away with Kolya. Now all that work seems like such a waste.

I brought it up with Kolya, who said it was up to me what I wanted to do with the rest of my life. He said I could work for him if I wanted, or I could set up a charity to run. He suggested doing something to help those leaving care—I thought that would be a worthwhile cause.

One thing we did decide on was contraception. After we'd had unprotected sex for the second night in a row, I asked if we could use something. I explained that I just wasn't ready to be a mum and would like to build our relationship before we brought a baby into the world. Kolya agreed, and ever since then, we'd been using condoms until I could go on the pill.

"You seem lost in thought, beautiful Tess. Is our conversation so unriveting that you're daydreaming to avoid it?" Yannis asked.

"Maybe," I teased.

"Kolya, I vote we take your wife out dancing again. Where do you suggest we go?"

We'd gone out to a club in London a couple of nights ago, and Yannis had insisted on dancing with me as often as possible. It was the first time I'd ever been to a nightclub. I'm glad it was with Kolya. Being under eighteen, I wouldn't be allowed in otherwise.

The club was owned by someone he knew, so we were allowed to hang out in the VIP section, along with well-known footballers, models, and singers. I'd felt a little over-awed at first. Yannis knew quite a few of them and introduced me to as many as he could in between drinking and dancing. I'll admit to being embarrassingly tongue-tied when speaking to them, but none seemed to have the airs and graces I expected of someone famous, and not one of them had as many guards as Kolya.

I wondered if our security team intimidated them. Though they tried to stay in the shadows, it was hard to miss Jonesy, Nate, Dave, and Lucas. Yannis only brought one guard, Deo, and had teased Kolya for insisting on bringing so many. Kolya scowled at Yannis and said the last time he'd taken security advice from him, there'd been an attempt on his life, and I'd ended up on the receiving end of the bullet.

That had been the only sour point of the night; the rest of it was amazing. An experience I'll never forget.

"Where would you like to go, Tess?" Kolya asked.

"It's all new to me, Kolya. I don't know where to suggest, and you seem to know all the best places."

He tugged me onto his lap and gave me a quick kiss on the lips. Kolya wasn't shy about showing his affection for me in public, but I wasn't that keen on it. I didn't mind holding hands, but Kolya's kisses had quite an effect on me, and I didn't like people seeing me so flustered.

He picked up his phone to see what was on locally; none of us felt like travelling to London. Of course, any day or evening out had to be planned with security in mind, so it wasn't as simple as just choosing what we fancied doing. I leaned against his shoulder, watching him scroll through a list of evening events around Oxford when a call came through from PC Foster. I stiffened, dreading whatever she had to say.

Kolya let it ring for a couple of seconds before answering. As I was sitting on his lap, I heard every word that was spoken, although I almost wished I hadn't.

PC Foster informed him they'd released Sarah's body for burial.

The conversation lasted less than three minutes, but it was enough to send my previously happy thoughts into a cold, dark place. Feelings of dread and a veil of sadness surrounded me.

It would be so easy to give in to my grief once again. Kolya would organise everything while I sat around and cried. But that wouldn't be right. I had to sort this out, and I needed to be strong for Jean, and Sarah.

Kolya told PC Foster that Jean and I wanted Sarah's body to be cremated. We were worried that one of the accused's friends or family might attack a grave, so I suggested we have her cremated so we could scatter her ashes in the loch at Glengarran. It was such a beautiful, peaceful place. Jean and I could go there and talk to her anytime we wanted while looking out over the water.

In the meantime, we had to arrange her funeral service. I knew from a previous conversation with PC Foster that both she and PC Winters—as well as Detectives Dickhead and Twatface—would be there, along with staff from The Willows and social services. I wanted to do something that showed them the beautiful, fun-loving girl that Sarah had been when we were living with Jean. When she'd finally had a family that cared for her the way she should have had all those years before. I needed them to see the happy, smiling face of a girl that had her whole life in front of her before the system failed her. Maybe by doing that, I could make them try harder with other kids in care.

Chapter Twenty-Seven

TESS

Choosing Sarah's coffin was so difficult. Jean wanted the same funeral directors she'd had when her husband died. The staff at Denton's Funeral Home were so patient and understanding, and I could see why she'd wanted to use them again.

It had taken a few days to get the approval for a cremation. After a murder or a death in suspicious circumstances, the coroner and police prefer a burial, in case they ever come across more evidence. With a burial, they can always exhume the body, but they'd already performed the only autopsy they could on Sarah due to the state of decomposition. I wondered how many they'd need to do on Hassan Akbar's body.

After looking at the various coffins at the undertaker's, I became so disheartened. Jean suggested we had a white one or pale oak. As Kolya was paying for it, money wasn't an issue, so one of the younger funeral directors brought out a catalogue containing coffins we could special order. We chose one in blush pink with a slightly sparkly effect. It reminded us of Sarah's favourite top that Jean bought her for her birthday. She'd worn it nearly every day for a month. Jean used to wash it in the morning and have it ready for Sarah to wear when she came home from school. It really suited her and went with just about everything.

When we went to The Willows, it went missing. Sarah was so upset about it and had cried for days before finding out one of the lads had ripped it. He was much bigger than her, but she didn't care. She gave him two black eyes and a split lip before the staff managed to pull her off him, and then I kicked him in the balls for good measure. He didn't steal anything else of hers or mine after that.

I didn't want a hearse to carry her coffin from Jean's house to the crematorium, so I asked if we could have a Cinderella-style carriage for her final journey through Doncaster. It seemed more appropriate. After all, we'd be scattering her ashes in front of a castle; it was only right that she arrived at her funeral like a princess.

Even with the extra money Kolya paid to ensure we got everything we asked for, it still took eleven days until we could have the cremation. It gave me plenty of time to sort something out for the funeral service.

Every single one of Kolya's guards said they'd be honoured to be a pallbearer. I can't even begin to tell you how much that meant to me. Jean had cried like a baby and fell in love with each and every one of them. It wasn't practical for Kolya to do it, though I know he wanted to, and Jonesy said we'd need at least three guards on close protection detail due to the crematorium being so exposed. Ivan had also offered to carry Sarah, but he was much taller than the rest of them, so she wouldn't have been evenly balanced.

In the end, we decided that Danny, Jonesy, Nate, and

Franco would carry her, and Ivan, Lucas, Dave and Kevin would be working close protection during the service.

Nan and Jack had insisted on coming, too, as did Yannis. He'd returned to Greece a few days ago but said he wanted to support me, just like everyone else. I was so touched by the outpouring of love and support I'd received from everyone that I'd been shedding tears daily. I know that's a natural reaction in a situation like this, but for what I planned to do at the service, it just wasn't helping.

Jean and I had been going through some videos she'd filmed when we'd lived with her. Sarah loved to sing, so Jean had bought her a karaoke game for the PlayStation she'd given her for Christmas. We'd pretend to introduce her on *The X Factor* and would respond with some of the regular judges' comments after she'd sung. We used to have a right giggle doing that.

Sarah had such a beautiful voice. I loved listening to her, but it was hard to watch those videos now.

When I'd shown the videos to Kolya and the guys, Sarah's natural vocal talent had blown them away. And yeah, they'd all had a good laugh at my fourteen-year-old self as Sarah's backing singer. Not that I'm a bad singer; I can certainly hold a tune. Yet compared to Sarah, I was severely lacking. Nevertheless, she nearly always included me in her songs.

There was one song she'd insisted on singing solo, and that was the first video I wanted to play at her funeral. The trouble was that the song was so emotional I'd crumble as soon as it began.

Kolya knew how much it affected me, and it hurt him to see me cry whenever I played it. He said I should pick something else. There were enough videos to choose from, but I knew they wouldn't have the same impact on the attendees as this one. Ivan was no help, either. Every time he saw me cry, he teared up too, which made me cry even more.

I glanced down at the words I'd written and shook my head. This was never going to work. There was so much I wanted to say, but I didn't know if I had the strength to stand there in front of everyone. Sarah's funeral was just hours away, and I was still a blubbering mess whenever I read the words out loud. I grabbed a tissue and blew my nose, feeling the beginnings of yet another headache.

Kolya had gone to London for a meeting and had taken Ivan, Jonesy, Nate, and, surprisingly, Danny. Kevin and his assistant were updating the security system, so all the cameras were off for the next few hours. I was glad. I didn't want an audience today.

Bess had been keeping me company in our TV room, and I knew my tears were upsetting her, but it couldn't be helped. The little wire-haired terrier whined and licked my face, trying to comfort me as best she could.

"You done upsetting the dog?" Franco asked. He'd been back less than a week, but he didn't look happy about it. I couldn't blame him. The mood in our home had been extremely sombre with all the funeral preparations.

"I've been practising reading the words I've written. When I'm a few lines in, I get a lump in my throat and can't seem to speak. Then I cry all over again. Kolya said I don't have to read it, but it's important that I get the words out there. They need to know they did wrong by her. What should I do, Franco?"

"You should start by being you, Tess. Not the whiney-ass

child they're all treating you like. You really wanna stand up there and be strong? To smack 'em in the face with words that'll make an impact about a girl they should never forget?" he questioned.

"You know I do," I replied.

"Then you need to toughen up. Stop looking at your husband for support. He can't help you with this. The Tess I met all those months ago didn't have to rely on a man for emotional support. Sure, you took it when it was offered, but you didn't need it."

"I'm a different person now, Franco. And I like the love and support he gives me. It's not something I ever expected, but I wouldn't change it. Not for the world."

"But that love and support comes from a man who would happily have you change something you want to keep so that he doesn't have to see you cry," he argued.

"It breaks his heart to see me so upset. I'd be the same if our roles were reversed," I told him.

"Then you'd be wrong, too." He glared at me as he said this. As if he expected me to challenge him, but I didn't have it in me.

Bess heard the clatter of plates in the kitchen and knew it was time to eat. She yipped and ran out of the door with her tail wagging.

We were travelling up to Doncaster later so we could be with Jean tonight. Sarah's funeral was at eleven in the morning, so we needed to be up and ready.

"Where's the girl that was gonna rip Caroline Dawson a new one? Has she gone already? Did the boss take away your fight when he took your cherry?" he taunted.

"Fuck you, Franco!" I jumped up from the sofa and began pacing.

"You offering, baby?" he questioned with a smirk. He

stepped towards me and put his hands on my arms, pinning them to my sides.

"Fight me, Tess. Here, right now. Show me how easily you can put me on my ass."

"Again, fuck you, Franco," I yelled, struggling to get out of his hold.

"That's the second time you've said that. What's up, Tess? Ain't the boss making the stars shine a little brighter for you when you go to bed at night?"

I used the self-defence moves he and Jonesy had taught me to get out of his hold, but he'd anticipated that and countered them with swift moves of his own, dropping me to my knees in front of him.

"You've been too long out of the ring, Tess. I used to think you'd be able to stand your ground and fight if a situation ever arose, but I guess you'd be better off running away—somewhere you can have a good cry about how weak you've become."

"I'll show you weak, you arsehole," I muttered as I struck out at his groin. His quick reaction stopped my fist from connecting with his balls, just as I knew it would. I couldn't understand why he was doing this, but I was seriously pissed off about it. I spun around and sideswiped his legs—a move that was new to me. He dropped to the rug and took me with him in a roll, pinning me down with his arm across my throat. I fucking hated this position, and he knew it. Barely taking two seconds to breathe, I turned my head to the right at the same time as I grabbed his ear and pulled, lifting my knees when he altered position. I used my feet to push him away and flipped us over, pinning *him* down this time.

"There's my girl," he declared. "You ain't lost your fire, Tess. It's right there, burning bright in your eyes. You got everything you need to stand there tomorrow and tell them fuckers whatever you want without crying. And if you feel yourself breaking, let your eyes find mine and remember how you took me down today. Those pansy-assed cops got nothin' on me, but you can't go brawling with 'em in that place. You gotta take 'em down with your emotional strength and use words instead. We can catch the bastards later when they least expect it and Taser 'em till they piss and shit themselves. How 'bout it, baby? Does that sound like a good plan to you?"

"You did this to help me?" I questioned incredulously. He grinned and raised one eyebrow in that tauntingly sexy way.

"Did it work?" he asked.

He laughed loudly while casually placing his hands behind his head.

"I don't know why I asked," he said. "Of course it worked! I'm a fucking genius with psychological shit like this. You know what, Tess? I think I missed my calling. I shoulda been a fucking shrink!" He laughed again, harder this time, and God help me, I couldn't help but laugh along with him.

"You're mad, you know that, Franco? Absolutely barking. And you've got to stop all the flirty, dirty, teasing remarks and calling me baby. You know Kolya will go apeshit if he hears you," I told him.

"Says the woman who's been straddling me for the last five minutes," he said, raising his eyebrows and bumping me up with his hips.

I gasped and leapt away from him as quickly as I could, thankful that the cameras were off today.

Chapter Twenty-Eight

TESS

I was so glad that the rain held off, although the dull grey sky looked as bleak as my mood.

Nan had made four large chiffon and silk bows in the same blush pink as Sarah's coffin, which she attached to the finials on each corner of the white carriage when it arrived outside Jean's house. Nan had sourced the same-coloured ties for each pallbearer, and one for Kolya.

Blush pink carnations surrounded Sarah's coffin, and matching floral displays of musical notes and the word SISTER lay on the roof of the carriage. Two white horses pulled the fairy-tale conveyance along at a steady pace.

We followed behind in three of Kolya's best cars, and I noticed several other vehicles behind ours.

Jean had planned the route to the crematorium, which took us past our school. I hadn't expected to find the entire school lining the pavements as we went by. All those pupils bowing their heads in a mark of respect brought a lump to my throat, and seeing her name in white flowers being held by her former teachers brought about my first tears of the day.

As our journey progressed, we headed down a familiar road. My stomach churned as we approached The Willows and I felt somewhat betrayed by Jean at that moment, but when I saw the tearful faces of some of the younger children who waited outside the gates, my feelings quickly changed. Each held a pink flower and a string of paper cut-outs of musical notes. Jean must have told them what we were surrounding Sarah with today. Their efforts were simple but touching.

I didn't see Lisa and Ben, but the rest of the staff were there, even those who only worked nights. Some were crying openly. My heart felt like it was being squeezed, and I had an overwhelming urge to stop the car so I could comfort them. I didn't know how to process that, but I knew I felt sorry for those I'd left behind. They would never get the chances in life that I had now.

The need to set up a charity for kids leaving care grew by the minute as we made our way up the winding road to the chapel at the crematorium.

When the carriage and cars came to a stop, I cleared my throat and glanced at everyone in the car. Jean had been sobbing since we passed the school, and though I'd held her hand, it was Ivan who dried her tears when we exited the vehicle. I knew if I'd turned to her and made eye contact, I'd have lost my nerve and would have been a complete mess by the time we arrived.

Kolya held my hand and kissed my fingers at various points along our journey. Still, again, I'd not made eye contact with him, and I'd not said a word to anyone, although I'd listened in to their conversation, nodding my head in agreement when necessary.

The undertakers had been apprised of the protocol surrounding Kolya. They waited for the guards to ensure that we were safely out of the vehicle before opening the doors to the carriage. Nan and Yannis came over to hug me, and that's when the tears began to fall.

Kolya pulled me into his arms and held me tightly, stroking my hair while saying he was proud of me for holding up so well. He said it was okay to cry, and I could rely on him to get me through today.

But it wasn't okay to cry. Not while I had something so important that needed to be said.

I looked around for Franco, needing his strength to carry me through the next thirty minutes, but I couldn't see him anywhere.

People were gathering on either side of the doors of the chapel. I noticed Ben from The Willows, who was holding Lisa's hand. Both she and Andrea, my old case worker, looked like they were crying. PC Foster and PC Winters stood behind them. I couldn't see the detectives, but I knew they were there. I had that familiar feeling of revulsion I got whenever they were around. You don't need to see shit to smell it.

"Can I have a minute with your wife, boss?" The relief I felt upon hearing Franco's voice was immense. Kolya let go of my hand but watched us closely until an undertaker approached him.

"Franco, I don't—OW! What was that for?" I questioned while rubbing the painful area above my hip bone where he'd just nipped me.

"Does it hurt?" he asked innocently.

"Of course it hurts. You just nipped me," I declared through my tears.

"Good. It needs to hurt."

"Why?" I asked, confused and thoroughly pissed off.

"Think of it as a positive hurt. If you feel you can't cope when it's time to get up there and do your thing, just give this a push," he said while poking the area he'd nipped, causing me to wince. "It will help distract you from what's going on so you can focus on what you need to do."

Jonesy approached us and placed a hand on Franco's shoulder, telling him they were ready. I watched them walk over to the carriage, along with Danny and Nate. They all wore black suits with white shirts, making their pink ties stand out. I hoped Sarah could see how much effort everyone had made for her today.

More people were joining us by the minute, and it surprised me how many had turned up. Her teachers arrived and handed over the floral display of her name to one of the undertakers. They looked like they wanted to come and speak to me, but that would have to wait.

Jean and Kolya came to stand by my side, and I watched with bated breath as the men who meant so much to me carried my beloved foster sister into the chapel.

I heard people crying and sniffling as they followed our sombre procession and found their seats. A four-foot projection of the best photograph of Sarah that Jean and I could find was displayed on a screen behind her coffin. Sarah had on her favourite top, and her smile lit up her pretty face.

She hadn't been christened or baptised, so the funeral director organised for a lay preacher they'd used before to conduct the service. I wasn't sure what denomination he was. When we met him last week, I never thought to ask. It wasn't important, anyway.

The preacher's name was Daniel, and he'd spoken to Jean and me at length about what we wanted for Sarah's funeral. We told him about all the happy times we'd shared with Sarah and how talented and funny she was. Then we talked about her abusive past and the events leading up to her death. When I told him what I wanted to say, he asked me to think very carefully about why I wanted to do it and who it would benefit or hurt. He must have been satisfied with my answer because he was completely on board with my plans.

Daniel began by introducing himself, telling everyone in attendance that he was honoured to have been asked to lead the service, which was a celebration of the life of Sarah Crowther, a much-loved foster daughter and sister, and the greatest, most loyal friend anyone could wish to have.

Jean and I hadn't seen eye to eye in the beginning when I'd asked Daniel to talk about Sarah's past, but she soon came around when he'd put his spin on things. Still, I felt her tense beside me when he took a deep breath and looked at her photograph.

"The carefree teenager in this photograph had little in her childhood to make her smile. Her parents were abusive, and Sarah suffered numerous beatings from being a toddler, some of which left her with broken bones, though her parents blamed their daughter's clumsiness whenever questioned. Even though she was placed on the at-risk register, Sarah's abuse continued for many years."

Daniel paused and looked around at the silent congregation.

"You would think that her life experiences would have made her introverted, unsociable—unable to accept or express love—that couldn't be further from the truth. Though I'm told Sarah had a quick temper, she also had a big heart and longed to be part of a loving family.

"Due to the kindness and understanding of a local fosterer, Jean Brent, Sarah not only found someone she came to call Mum, but she also gained a sister in Tess." Daniel gestured towards me.

This was it! As we stood, I took a deep, steadying breath, gripping Kolya's bicep. He escorted me to the small pulpit at the side of the altar that Daniel had vacated before returning to his seat. I had a sheet of paper in my pocket, and though I didn't yet need it, my fingers clasped it nervously. In front of me was a remote control that belonged to a projector. It was already set up with what I needed; Kevin had made sure of it.

I looked out at the congregation and smiled at everyone. Some deserved it; they'd been kind to Sarah and me. Others most certainly did not.

"Before I say a few words, I'd like to show you a happy memory that Jean and I have of Sarah. It's one of many. While this video is playing, I'd like you to see what we saw every time we looked at her. A wonderful girl who was full of smiles and love. A girl desperate to share her life with people who'd return that love unconditionally."

I pressed play on the remote control and watched as her photograph vanished from view. I appeared in its place, welcoming a twelve-year-old Sarah to our makeshift stage—the bay window area in Jean's front room. After the first few notes from the piano, I turned to watch the expressions on the faces of the congregation. Sarah began singing Birdy's version of "Skinny Love"—her pitch hauntingly beautiful. Perfect as it always was.

From where I stood, the left side of the small congregation was made up of representatives from social services and the local police force. Along the front row was a tearful Lisa and red-eyed Ben. Next to them were our caseworkers, Andrea and Gill. PCs Winters and Foster stood beside them, wiping their eyes as they watched Sarah become lost in the soulful song.

Detectives Dickhead and Twatface were on the row behind. Both looked uncomfortable, and it was clear to see they'd rather be anywhere else but here. They kept glancing over to the other side of the chapel where my husband and Ivan were comforting Jean. Our guards were on the row behind, along with Yannis and his guards, Deo and Ezio. My eyes flicked back to Franco for a moment before moving along.

Jean's neighbours, Mr and Mrs Hancock, stood with four of Sarah's teachers. All were wiping their eyes while trying to smile as the video progressed, likely trying to lock the images away so they could replace the terrible thoughts they might have about how she died. I could understand that. It was one of the reasons I'd put so much thought into her coffin. I'd seen the photographs of her long-dead body and wanted to replace those images with ones that didn't give me nightmares. So I picked the highest quality pale pink taffeta to line her coffin and asked them to cover her in pink satin. Of course, no one would get to see it, but that wasn't the point. Sarah deserved the very best—whether in life or death. Being with Kolya had given me the means to provide the latter.

There were a few more people I didn't recognise, though I thought one or two could be journalists. PC Foster had warned us we might get a few today, but I wouldn't have made them leave even if she'd suggested it. I needed them for what I had to do next.

As the song ended, Sarah waited with exaggerated nervousness for the *judge's* response. In the video, Jean cleared her throat before declaring, "I didn't like that performance, Sarah... I loved it! I think we've found this year's winner." The congregation laughed as Sarah and I jumped up and down while hugging each other.

Kevin had captured the last frame of the video in a still shot. In it, Sarah was smiling and hugging me. I kept that shot instead of replacing it with the photograph, though I began to rethink my decision when I looked at it for a few seconds longer than planned. Tears rolled down my cheeks, so I reached into my pocket for a tissue, pulling out the piece of paper at the same time.

I wiped my eyes and nose, then looked over at Franco, who pointed his finger sideways, reminding me to poke the area he'd nipped. While it didn't feel as bad as when he'd done it, it helped me focus.

"Sarah had such a beautiful voice, didn't she? I still can't believe she's gone."

I took a moment to acknowledge some of the attendees.

"Miss Wilson, you were Sarah's favourite teacher. She was so good at maths. Even though I was older, Sarah often helped me with my homework. When we got to The Willows, she helped the younger kids with their maths homework, too. But then again, she did that a lot—help people, I mean. Especially those who couldn't help themselves, like kids who were being bullied in school or at The Willows. Sarah always got in trouble for it, but she didn't care. She thought beating bullies was the right thing to do. Sarah said it was worth having detention or getting grounded to know she'd given a bully a taste of their own medicine. I think she enjoyed fighting for those who couldn't, for whatever reason, fight for themselves. After all, that had been her when she was younger, though the bullies in that situation had been her parents.

"Does that give you all a different perspective on why Sarah fought so much?" I asked as I looked around the room. I took another deep breath and continued. "The thing that hurts the most is…she didn't have many people willing to fight for her.

"From day one, she was left with abusive, drug-addicted parents. There were so many red-flag occasions that were ignored. Doctors reported every hospital admission to social services, but it took years and her mother dying for her to escape that hell… failure number one.

"When Jean had her heart attack, they took us straight to The Willows. No one sat us down and told us how long we had to stay there—or let us know what was happening to our foster mum. We were so worried about Jean, and we thought we might never get to see her again. No wonder Sarah rebelled.

"A different approach might have made the transition from foster family to residential children's home an easier pill to swallow. But no one saw it from our side. Not to our knowledge, anyway. I've since learned how much effort Lisa put into trying to help us visit Jean. For that, I'm truly grateful."

Lisa looked shocked by my admission but nodded at my acceptance of her efforts.

"Preventing Jean's access to us at The Willows, along with the way we were left there, was yet another failure. But it wouldn't be the last.

"When I went to my tutor, Mrs Keating, and let her know what Sarah told me was happening with Farid, Hassan, and Tariq, they took her away from The Willows to a temporary home across town. It was the right thing to do, yet she was only gone for five days. Why? Why couldn't she have been kept there and watched? She should have been able to confide in someone and maybe receive counselling. Why couldn't the police have arrested Farid, Hassan, and

Tariq? How bad does a crime against children have to be to make you act?" I questioned loudly while staring at the detectives. One of them shifted nervously while the other, Detective Constable Twatface/Twain, glared at me defiantly. He wasn't the slightest bit bothered that Sarah was dead.

"Something I came to realise many years ago...kids like Sarah and me don't matter. Our parents might be drunks or junkies or both. Maybe they're selling sex to buy illegal substances because they care about getting high more than they care for us. Perhaps they're habitual thieves or people who collect antisocial behaviour convictions like they're going out of fashion. The automatic response to us seems to be, *'Why waste time on them? They'll never amount to anything.'* It's like we don't deserve the same thought, care, and respect as children born to regular, hardworking parents. Those that fit into the ideal of what a conventional family should be.

"It doesn't matter how well-behaved we are or how smart we might be. Our cards are already marked. We're an inconvenience. We'll be on drugs and on the game like our mums. We must be lying when we say people are hurting us. And it's obvious we're being racist when we tell you that a gang of Pakistani men are raping our friends. Isn't that so, Detective Constable Dickson and Detective Constable Twain? I call that a failure of epic proportions."

They both looked like they were about to object, but PC Winters gave them a warning glare, shaking his head to reinforce his silent message.

"How many more young lives will be ruined before those that should have protected them take responsibility for their failures? What will it take to change the system to protect the vulnerable?

"There are monsters out there who search out their

victims carefully. They prey on those they consider easy targets: children who desperately need consistency and love in their lives. Children who lack the material things that some of their peers take for granted.

"Tariq Akbar was a DJ at the local youth club. Presumably, he'd had to undergo police checks and fill in a disclosure form before he could work with kids. Of course, he had every right to take that job if nothing had been flagged on his police check. But what about afterwards? The rest of the staff knew how friendly he was with the girls. How Sarah, Beth, and others their age hung around him. They must have seen him give some of those girls a lift home. Maybe they were like me: they knew something was off, but because the girls were behaving themselves in public, they let it go. Treated it like a passing phase.

"You see, I failed Sarah too. I knew that something wasn't quite right, but I said and did nothing because Sarah had stopped getting into trouble so much. By the time I found out what was going on, it was already too late. Those men had got their claws into Sarah. Farid Ali convinced her she was special to him, that he loved her and wanted her to be his for always. For someone who craved love and affection, you can see how easily he and his gang manipulated her.

"They gave the girls phones. Sarah thought that meant they were kind and generous when really it was a way to keep control over them and their whereabouts. Sarah tried to end it, but they threatened Jean and me—people who meant more to her than anything. They showed her photos of me leaving school and Jean outside her house. She was scared they would hurt us if she told anyone. And let's face it…when any of them *did* inform the police, the information went nowhere. The groomers could rely on the police to ignore their victims."

I let out a sarcastic laugh, then stared at the despicable detectives before saying, "There you go, fellas. At least some members of society can rely on you.

"Some of you might think a funeral isn't the right time or place to bring all this up. I think it's the perfect time. When I first began talking about Sarah, I mentioned how she'd fight for others. She cared about people and would stand up for them as best she could. She can't do that now —not physically, anyway. By getting everyone to talk about what happened to Sarah—not only what led to her death, but throughout her short life—then maybe lessons can be learned that will prevent those failures from happening to another vulnerable child. My husband has suggested I set up a charity to help young people leaving care. I think that's a great idea. But I also think we should extend the umbrella of that charity to other children who are in a no-win situation because of their upbringing. I'd like to call the charity Sarah's Legacy. It will be a way of keeping her name and memory alive. A way she can still fight for those that need her help.

"The charity will give young people chances in life they might otherwise be denied—a way for them to secure a brighter future. It could help with further education or getting a place to live or work.

"Many of you are involved with children and young people professionally. You would be more than welcome to send me suggestions of how you think the charity could help those in need. My husband's business will be the charity's main benefactor, though I'm hoping we can eventually rely on public donations and support."

I looked towards Sarah's coffin, noticing for the first

time how the sparkles in the paintwork reflected the light from the stained-glass windows.

"Sarah's ashes will be scattered in the loch at Glengarran Castle in the Scottish Highlands. My husband and I got married there, so it means a lot to me. As he owns the castle and the land surrounding it, he asked me to let you know that you're welcome to visit her final resting place whenever you're in the area. If you let us know beforehand, we can inform the staff, who will be happy to greet you upon your arrival."

I recalled Mrs Braeburn, the housekeeper at Glengarran, and thought the last sentence might not strictly be true. She hadn't been so welcoming to me.

"I'd like to thank you all for coming here today. Seeing everyone outside school and The Willows paying their respects meant a lot to Jean and me. There's a small buffet and refreshments in the tearoom at the bottom of the hill if anyone would like to join us.

"Before we leave, I'd like to play you one last video of Sarah. It includes me, too, so I'll apologise beforehand for my less-than-stellar voice."

I pressed play on the remote control again and waited for the next video. It was of both of us singing "Wings," another of Birdy's songs and one of my favourites.

Kolya came forward and took my arm as I stepped down from the pulpit before escorting me back to my seat beside Jean. During the last chorus of "Wings," the dark blue heavy velvet curtains on either side of the altar closed, removing Sarah's coffin and the video from our view.

Chapter Twenty-Nine

KOLYA

No one could stay long at the customary funeral buffet. Teachers had to return to classes, and PCs Foster and Winters were getting ready for the afternoon shift.

Before she left, PC Foster informed us that Farid Ali had been spotted at a mosque with Hassan Akbar the night he'd been reported missing. Apparently, Farid had also been spotted buying kebabs at a takeaway in Leeds, so the police were working on the assumption that he was hiding in West Yorkshire. The officer wanted us to be aware in case we were planning on spending time in the area.

Tess had kept her expression blank, her confusion masked. She knew Farid Ali was dead. She also knew it was me who'd killed him. Although she'd met Rashid, Tess hadn't noticed his resemblance to Farid—or maybe she *had* noticed but hadn't wanted to acknowledge it. I was thankful that Rashid hadn't joined us today and wondered if he'd be willing to shave off his beard.

The two detectives my wife despised hadn't attended the buffet. I was glad about that. I wanted to hurt them. Badly.

Their treatment of Tess was unacceptable. I thought that shit involving Carrick would have stuck to them, too, but they'd been lucky so far. Before the year is out, I will ensure their careers are ruined.

Teachers from Tess's school said they would be happy to support the charity she had proposed, as did PC Foster. Neither Tess nor I could discuss it further until we had the legal side sorted, which everyone understood. I'd spoken with Oliver Ward-Jones about the project, and he was handing it over to his associate to deal with. I promised everyone we'd be in touch when we heard from the Charities Commission. In the meantime, we were open to any ideas. I suggested we set up a meeting to discuss our mission statement once the charity had been registered.

Yannis had left as soon as the service was over. Before he and his team drove away, he'd placed a gift in our vehicle for Tess. He had a meeting in Paris that couldn't be postponed, but he promised he'd call her later to see how she was. Tess had won him over with little effort. He admired her wit, outspokenness, and bravery.

Yannis and Catherine had already been good friends when we met. It was he who introduced us. They'd never had a cross word or heated debate in all the years they'd known each other. I could not say the same.

Yannis and I had often argued. Sometimes we'd go weeks without speaking if he was in one of his sulks, though it was never serious enough to break our friendship. I doubt anything could do that. We were like brothers, he and I.

Catherine said that Yannis was mollycoddled by his parents in his younger years. He was an only child and had been used to getting his own way, which was something she had understood. As an adult, he wanted to do the same, but that's not always acceptable. He always let James have his way and gave him everything he asked for—often berating Catherine and me if we denied him anything.

The last time Yannis and I had a blazing row was on New Year's Day. We were both hungover, and he was unhappy that I'd decided against buying one of his company's shipyards. It had been out of commission for some time, and he'd offered me the chance to purchase the shipyard and the surrounding land for a significantly reduced price. The proposal was appealing, but I'd already decided to buy in central or northern Europe due to the attractive incentives the EU was offering. He'd stormed out of my hotel and refused to speak to me for a couple of months, although I knew he kept in contact with James.

Yannis rang me at the end of February and apologised for his behaviour. I accepted his apology, and he assured me the argument would be forgotten.

When we met up again in April, our friendship was the same as it always was. We were going to have a late dinner, then hit a club. Yannis told me he was in the mood for a night of debauchery with a beautiful stranger as we made our way out of the building. Then chaos erupted around us, and an angel with wild copper-coloured hair saved my life, risking her own in turn.

I watched my angel from across the room. It looked like she was in a heated discussion with one of her old social workers. I made my way across to her, smiling as I pondered the thought of Tess and Yannis arguing. I knew my wife wouldn't put up with his childish sulks. They both had a quick temper, but my friend wouldn't stand a chance against her when she was out for blood.

"Is there a problem here, ladies?" I slipped my arm around Tess and stared at the woman she'd disagreed with.

"Andrea here is being all judgy, as per usual. She said

she's concerned about my welfare and offered to help me get away from you."

"Is that so?" I replied, my voice calm and steady, though inside, I was furious.

Andrea stuck her chin in the air and stared at me defiantly.

"I was only offering Tess another option. I wanted her to know our department could still help her," she said rather loudly as if she wanted everyone to hear.

Franco and Jonesy laughed out loud at her bold statement.

"Now they want to help! Too late for that poor girl we carried into the chapel today," commented Franco, and I wholeheartedly agreed.

"Apart from dealing with the events surrounding Sarah's death, I'm happier than I've ever been in my whole life. But you refuse to acknowledge that, Andrea," Tess declared.

"All you see is a man who is older than me—a wealthy man who can have anything or anyone he wants, yet he chooses me. That sets off alarm bells in your head because, obviously, I'm no one special. An ex-foster kid with a troubled background. It's exactly what I said in the chapel. You can't see how I'd be suitable for someone like Kolya or how he could love me. So you look at Kolya and find flaws with him instead.

"You've already mentioned the age difference. You're assuming he's got a thing for young girls and probably think he has a whole harem waiting for him in Russia somewhere. You suggested he's not a good man because he creates and sells weapons, but some of those weapons are used by our military to keep our country and others safe. I went to a ball in London a few weeks ago and watched him speak with government ministers and foreign dignitaries. They know Kolya well and have a lot of respect for him.

"You also said you know what they are like. I'm confused by that sentence. Did you mean arms dealers, Russians, or just men in general? Let's go through them all, shall we?"

I heard Jonesy mutter, "She's on one now, God help us."

If Tess heard him, she didn't pause her angry tirade.

"Arms dealers are filthy rich and can talk the hind legs off a donkey when it comes to the next big thing in weaponry and defence, especially when they create the stuff.

"Next up, we'll take the fact that although Kolya has dual citizenship, he's Russian by birth. And we all know how the media likes to portray Russians. Homophobic, racist, intolerant of anything different. My husband isn't any of those things. Take Nate over there. He's of African American descent and lives with his other half, Kevin, in our home. Kevin also works for Kolya. And if you care to check, you'll discover he has other staff members from an ethnic or other minority.

"Now, let's talk about the fact that he's a man. You assume you know what all men are like—probably think he's sex mad and couldn't wait to get *'vulnerable little me'* into bed at the earliest opportunity. You couldn't be more wrong. Kolya valued and respected my innocence. Even though we were married, he said he wouldn't sleep with me until I turned eighteen, which drove me bloody mad. But I see what a good man that makes him, and I love him all the more for it.

"So you can keep your bigoted, judgemental attitude to yourself and go write up your little report of today's events. Remember to add that the man you dislike will do more for kids leaving care within the next twelve months than you'll have done in your whole career."

"Tess, Mr Barinov, I didn't mean—"

"Leave!" yelled a voice from behind me. I turned to find Jean glaring daggers at the social worker. If looks could kill, the woman would have died instantly.

"Jean, I swear to you, Tess has it all wrong. She misinterpreted what I'd said," Andrea stammered.

"I highly doubt that. Now, do as I said and leave. You are not welcome here. You and your department let Sarah down right from the start. You're a disgrace, the lot of you. If you need to be escorted out, this lovely young man will gladly show you the door," Jean told her, gesturing towards Ivan. His face was like thunder, his big, muscular arms folded tightly across his chest. Ivan's fierce blue eyes bore a hole in the blustering woman's forehead.

"There's, erm, no need, erm… I'm sorry," she said before dashing towards the door.

"Are you all right, love?" Jean asked as she took Tess in her arms, hugging her tightly.

"Yeah, I am now that she's gone. I was trying to keep my cool in here, but some of the things she said and what she was insinuating… Honestly, Jean, I felt like punching the bitch," Tess declared.

My wife was shaking with anger and frustration. I needed to get her away from the place before anyone else made any sly remarks.

"Jean, I think it's time that Tess and I left. Lucas, Kevin, and Nate will take you home. Kevin wants to check that your new security system is performing as it should."

Jean nodded, placing a finger over Tess's lips when she began to object.

"Go home, Tess. Get some rest. You're looking a bit peaky, love. Nan says you've not been eating much."

"I haven't felt like it, Jean. I've been so worried about today. Every time I try to eat something, I feel sick. I was worried that something would go wrong, but I think we did well by Sarah, didn't we?"

"We did, love. She'd have been proud of you today. And I know I've said it before, but I'm so grateful to you for your generosity, Kolya. She went out like a princess. I can't thank you enough."

Jean looked like she was going to cry again, so I hugged her and Tess together.

"It was my pleasure, Jean. Sarah is family—whether she is here with us or not. And I make sure my family has the very best. Always."

Mr Hancock stopped us on the way out. He'd taken some cuttings of the plants I'd admired in his garden when we'd stayed with Jean. He told me they were almost ready to be planted, so I arranged for Nate to collect them before they left.

The man's thoughtfulness was touching. It had taken time and effort to do that for me, so I thanked him profusely before promising to keep him updated on how they were doing.

Ivan drove us back to Oxford. Franco occupied the front passenger seat while Jonesy sat in the rear with us. We'd been driving a few minutes before I remembered the gift Yannis had left for Tess. I passed it to her and watched her open it.

"It's a mask," Tess stated as she took out the opulent disguise. The bevelled wooden stick was finished in antique gold and held a Venetian Colombina mask that covered her eyes, cheeks, and the bridge of her nose. Gold brocade lay over vibrant jewel colours in a diamond pattern. It was a quirky yet beautiful piece that suited my wife so well. Beneath the mask was a note that Tess read aloud.

"Though a woman as lovely as you should never hide her beauty, I thought you might like to wear this to the masquerade ball. With love, Yannis."

"The hoteliers' ball is being held in Paris this year. I thought we'd take in the sights beforehand." I'd forgotten to tell her about the ball, which was understandable with everything that had happened recently.

"Will that Dawson woman be there?" she asked, her pretty features full of distaste.

"I wouldn't worry about that, Tess. You could always clobber her with the mask if she is," Jonesy quipped. We all erupted into laughter, including Tess.

"You always find a way to lighten my mood, Jonesy," she told him.

"We could call for ice cream and chocolate, Tess, just to be on the safe side," he joked.

We all laughed again, though Tess's expression turned into one of confusion, followed by sheer panic. She closed her eyes and muttered something under her breath before counting the fingers of her right hand.

"Oh, shit!" she whispered.

"What is it, Tess? What's wrong?" I asked.

She opened her eyes and stared at me for a few seconds before saying, "I think we need to stop at a pharmacy before we get home."

Chapter Thirty

TESS

Eight and a half months later

My back was bloody killing me, but it was my own fault. Maybe Ivan's fault, too. After attending a couple of antenatal classes with me when Kolya was away, he'd struck up a conversation with a couple of women who'd used dance as a form of exercise in the late stages of pregnancy.

One woman said she thought dancing to *Tina Turner* songs had helped her baby's head engage, so Ivan put YouTube on the TV and joined me in nine minutes of Tina Turner-style dancing. We danced along to a concert performance of "Proud Mary." Twice! Franco and Rashid had been howling with laughter, but Ivan wasn't bothered in the slightest. He'd embraced everything about this pregnancy as if *he* was the expectant parent.

Our baby had already been spoiled beyond belief with all the toys, clothes, and nursery items we'd accumulated. I never knew there was so much stuff you had to buy for a new baby.

I stopped reading some of the pregnancy books I'd ordered because they scared me half to death, although Ivan had read them back-to-back. Kolya became fed up with him by the time I'd hit the five-month mark. Ivan still needed help with the translation of some English words, especially when reading.

Kolya and I decided we didn't want to know the sex of our baby until he or she was born, although some people thought we were mad not to. They'd be loved and cared for either way, so it really wasn't important.

Kolya's father had made it clear he wanted a boy. He said he wanted a child who could pass on the family name. Roman Barinov can be a bit of an arse sometimes, yet he seems to have a soft spot for me.

I met him in person after we'd been on our honeymoon. Kolya had taken me to a private island in the Caribbean. It was spectacular. The sand was almost white, and the sea was the most crystal-clear pale blue you could ever wish to see. I spent my eighteenth birthday jet-skiing throughout the day, followed by a party on the beach at night. Kolya even flew Jean and Nan out for a few days. Everyone made me feel like a pampered princess. It was perfect.

We'd spent two weeks on the paradise island before flying to Berlin and then Moscow. The rain and drop in temperature were a shock to the system after a fortnight of hot, sunny days.

Moscow was nothing like I thought it would be, though we only hit the tourist sights and his family home. I got on well with Kolya's brothers, especially his oldest brother, Yuri. Each of the brothers looked so alike, having the same ice-blue eyes as their father, yet none had his coldness. He was always so friendly with me and treated me like a daughter in a way. But I knew what he did for a living, so letting my guard down in his presence hadn't been easy at first. We speak via video call every couple of days now, and he called twice a day to check up on me when I had tonsillitis last month. Not at all how I expected a mafia boss to behave.

The pains in my back had been getting worse by the hour; even sitting down was uncomfortable. I walked across to the window and looked out over Mayfair, my hands pressing firmly against my lower back. The baby gave me a hard kick over on my right side. It seemed he or she was protesting about this morning's activities. I should have gone back to bed for an hour to get some rest.

We were staying at Kolya's Hotel in London because it was easier for us to get to the hospital from here. No NHS for baby Barinov and me. I'd be giving birth in The Lindo Wing at St Mary's Hospital, just like the Royals. Not bad for the orphaned ex-foster kid from Doncaster!

The back pain came on again, and I felt a tightening in my belly at the same time. I hitched in a breath, putting my hands on the windowsill to steady myself.

Shit! I knew what that was. I'd had the Braxton Hicks ones for the past week, but this was so much stronger.

I took out my phone and sent a text to Kolya.

I'm in labour. What time will you be done with your meeting?

Kolya was in Whitehall having a meeting with the Secretary of State for Defence, so I didn't expect him to reply straight away, but in less than a minute, I had an incoming text.

I'll end the meeting now and be on my way. How far apart are the contractions?

I felt a little foolish. I'd only had one.

No rush, Kolya; I've just had my first. Haven't told Ivan yet. Don't want him fussing, I replied.

How's the backache? Could it have been the start of labour? he questioned.

I was about to reply with, *"No. Tina Turner's to blame,"* when another contraction hit. It felt like someone was tightening a foot-wide elastic band around my whole abdomen. I groaned and placed my hand over my belly.

"I've got you, Tess." Franco slipped an arm under my bust and pulled me against him, my back to his chest. "Breathe through it, baby. That's it, nice and steady."

When the pain finally ebbed, I sagged against him in relief, then took out my phone.

Just had another contraction. It really hurts, Kolya.

"Was that your first contraction?" Franco asked, just as Ivan walked into the room.

"Contraction… YOU'RE HAVING CONTRACTIONS?" Ivan bellowed. He dashed towards me, picked me up, and then carried me to the sofa.

"It's my second big one, but I've had backache on and off for four hours. I thought I'd pulled it when I was dancing around this morning. I need to call the hospital. My contractions are about three minutes apart," I told them.

"THREE MINUTES?" Ivan yelled.

"Ivan, for fuck's sake. Stop with all the hollering. Tess doesn't need that right now," Franco told him.

"And the baby doesn't need to hear you swearing, Franco," Ivan admonished.

He'd read somewhere that babies in the womb could hear and recognise voices. Ivan had been like the swear police ever since.

He called the hospital and passed me the phone. Before I could tell the midwife what was happening, another contraction had me bending over as far as I could to cope with the pain. When it finally receded, I felt my underwear and maternity jeans becoming wet.

Ivan was relaying my details to the midwife over the phone. He'd made it his business to learn all my medical history, along with whatever the midwife had written in my antenatal booklet, so he was in a good position to speak for me until I signalled for him to pass me the phone.

"I think my waters broke, or I've wet myself, I'm not sure," I told the midwife in a panic. "I've had backache for hours, but I thought that was because of 'Proud Mary,'" I added.

"*Proud Mary?*" she questioned.

"The song," I replied. "We did it twice. I thought I'd pulled my back with all the dancing, but I must have been in labour. This is all happening way too quickly, and I'm just not ready for it. They said in antenatal class that first labours can go on for hours."

"*Mrs Barinov, the gentleman I spoke to said you are in Mayfair, which is only around eight to twelve minutes away, depending on traffic. Because your waters have broken and your contractions are only three minutes apart, I'd like to send an ambulance and midwife to you, just in case. The address we have for you is the penthouse suite at Lassiter's Hotel. Is that still correct?*" she asked.

"Yes, that's correct," I replied. "Will I have time to get a bath?"

"*Because your waters have broken, we'd rather you shower than get in the bath. Can you have your antenatal booklet ready for when the midwife arrives, along with anything you need for you and your baby during your stay? Your room will be ready for you when you arrive.*"

"Everything is ready to go. I just need to clean up and change my clothes," I told her.

After my next contraction had passed, Ivan walked me to the bedroom and then switched the shower on for me. He insisted I left the door to the bathroom open while I got myself cleaned up. I purposely didn't make a sound during my next contraction. I didn't want him to come to my aid and see me naked. And if he noticed the blood in my underwear, I thought he might freak. It was just a small amount, and I wasn't bleeding now.

I needed Ivan to be calm. Until Kolya got here, he was the only one who could do the deep breathing exercises with me.

It wasn't how bad the contractions were, but how long they lasted. I honestly thought they'd build up slowly and get stronger over time. I didn't know who to ask for advice. Jean hadn't had any children of her own, and Nan had gone to Covent Garden for lunch before going to see *Blood Brothers* in the West End. It was her birthday treat from her sister, so I didn't want to disturb her.

I knelt in the shower when I felt the familiar painful tightening once again. Holding the warm shower spray on my lower belly seemed to help, so I stayed there a while, letting the gentle heat do its thing until my knees began to ache.

I got out of the shower and put on my white towelling robe, hoping I wouldn't get blood on the back of it as I rinsed my underwear and jeans in cold water. I could still feel plenty of movement from the baby, which was reassuring.

My next contraction had me gripping the side of the sink, and I felt a little more fluid running down my leg when the pain subsided. Ivan knocked on the open door before stepping into the bathroom. His face seemed paler; his expression grim.

"Tess, there's been several incidents across London within the last ten minutes. It looks like a coordinated terrorist attack. There were gunshots outside Whitehall, so the building is on lockdown. Kolya hasn't been able to leave. We've spoken to Nan; she's at the theatre already, so she's safe. There's been a minor explosion on one of the roads leading to St Mary's Hospital, so the ambulance has been delayed until the police deem it safe. I've just spoken with one of the midwives again. They said to call if anything changes."

"Has anyone been hurt? Have you definitely spoken to Kolya?" I gripped Ivan's shirt and looked directly into his eyes to determine if he was telling the truth. As he was around sixteen inches taller than me, that wasn't an easy task.

"When you are done in here, you can call him yourself. Rashid is on the phone with him now. Do you need me to help you?"

"I need clean underwear and…something out of my hospital bag," I told him.

"What is it you want from the bag?" he asked.

I wanted him to bring me the maternity pads I'd packed for after I gave birth, but I felt too embarrassed to tell him —until another contraction came along. Then I almost growled out the words as I clung to him.

When the pain had passed, Ivan left to get what I'd requested from my bedroom. I wiped away the slow trickle of amniotic fluid that was running down my legs and threw the washcloth in the bath, along with my wet clothes. I didn't like putting wet things in the laundry hamper and wished we were at home in Oxford or at Glengarran.

Ivan came back into the bathroom and handed me one

197

of the huge maternity pads. Then he dropped to his knees and held my knickers open for me to step into.

"Ivan, what are you doing? You can't help me put my knickers on!" I exclaimed.

"I can, and I will. You can sort out the…thing," he said, gesturing to the pad in my hand. "Now hurry. As soon as you have your underwear on, you can come and get comfortable on the bed. We can do the breathing exercises and listen to music until we hear from Kolya or the midwife."

I placed the pad on the edge of the bath and stepped into my knickers carefully, one hand on his shoulder, the other making sure my bathrobe stayed closed. Ivan tugged them up until they were just past my knees, and then he got up and went back to the bedroom. I'd just got the pad in place when I felt the beginnings of another contraction. Sitting on the edge of the bath and rocking seemed to help with the pain, and as soon as it had passed, I went to the toilet and emptied my bladder again.

I heard a knock on the bedroom door before Franco said he was coming in. Ivan told him I was in the bathroom and would be out soon. Franco relayed the message back to someone else before saying, "No chance, boss. The last time was a one-off. I had no choice."

Franco sounded irritated. Angry, even. After washing my hands, I went into the bedroom to speak to Kolya. I needed to see him, so I suggested we video called. When the call connected and I finally saw him, he looked even more stressed than I did.

"Kolya, please don't worry about me. I'm about to listen to some music with Ivan, so it's all good, I promise."

"I cannot believe this is happening. I need to be with you, my darling. It's killing me to know you are in pain and can't turn to me for

comfort. But they won't let us go to our cars until they've been thoroughly checked." Kolya ran his hands through his hair and began pacing the room he was in, which looked like a library. I could see Jonesy following behind him, and there were other men in suits sitting on leather Chesterfield sofas.

"I'm fine, Kolya, honestly. I'm sure the—" I dropped the phone on the bed when a contraction that was worse than all the others rolled through my belly in never-ending waves.

"Aargh," I cried out in agony as the torturous tightening took my pain to another level. Ivan was yelling for me to take long, deep breaths—in through my nose, out through my mouth—but how could I when it felt like a boa constrictor had wrapped itself around my belly and was squeezing me to death?

"You will find a way to get me to my wife, or you can kiss goodbye to any further deals with my company, and I will close down every KOLCAT site in the UK," I heard Kolya shout.

Once the contraction had passed, I asked Ivan to help me get comfortable, then I called the midwife to tell her how intense the last pain was. I knew it wouldn't be long before the baby came, but in all the books and at all the classes, they said that labour, especially with first babies, took forever. Other women had been telling me how they killed time before they finally went to the hospital, and it had still taken hours once they got there. I was worried that something was going wrong because it was happening so quickly.

The midwife reassured me that everything was happening as it should. I didn't have excessive blood loss, and I wasn't feeling dizzy or suffering from a headache. I had another contraction while she was on the line, and it wasn't as painful as the last one, thank goodness.

Kolya called Franco again, and it sounded like he was pleading with him. Rashid came into the bedroom and said he'd spoken to the hotel manager, asking if there were any trained medical professionals staying at the hotel. Apparently, there was a doctor, but he was out. Just my luck. There were several staff who were trained first aiders, but then again, so were Ivan, Franco, and Rashid. I'd rather have people I knew than strangers looking after me. And let's face it, it wasn't a case of bandaging me up and putting me in the recovery position, was it? I know first aiders do so much more than that, but I was feeling aggravated and so bloody fed up. Even with all this money and privilege, things couldn't go right for me. I was cursed.

"What's going on with Franco and Kolya?" I whispered.

Ivan sat with his back against the headboard and moved me to sit between his legs. I lay back and rested my head against his chest.

"Franco delivered his nephew when his sister went into labour. Kolya said he might have to do the same for you if the ambulance doesn't arrive. Franco isn't too happy about it, as you can see."

Franco came towards the bed and touched my cheek.

"We were stuck eight floors up in a dirty, stinking elevator. It was the scariest moment of my life, and I did it because there was no other choice, Tess. I came to work for the boss a week later and got my sister out of that crappy apartment as soon as I could. I rented a small house in the suburbs for her until I had enough cash saved to buy one somewhere decent. My niece was born in a good hospital, twenty minutes from where they live. Which is where you should be right now."

Another contraction came along, and I managed to breathe through it with Ivan until I was about midway through, then the pain became too much, and I cried out. I could hear Kolya on Franco's phone, swearing like crazy, but I couldn't deal with him right now.

"That was less than two minutes since the last one," Ivan stated.

"I fucking know that, Ivan," I declared.

"No swearing in front of the baby, Tess," he chided.

"Ivan, for God's sake, give it a rest!" Rashid grumbled. He came to sit beside us.

"As far as we are aware, there were five separate incidents across the city. Two small explosions and suspected gunfire in three different locations, so it might be some time before the roads are cleared. And we can't fly you to a hospital because whenever there's a terrorist incident, the capital becomes a no-fly zone to all aircraft—other than air ambulances and high-ranking government evacuations. We have another bulletproof vehicle on standby, but because there've been explosions, we feel it would be unsafe to transport you to the hospital until the threat to the city has been contained."

I nodded in agreement and then squeezed his hand when the next contraction came. They seemed to last a little longer each time, and I could feel so much pressure down below.

"We should get the midwife on the phone again," I told them. "I think I'll need to push soon."

Franco called through to the hospital and passed me the phone.

"How do I know if I need to push?" I questioned nervously. Before she could answer, I told her about the contractions being less than two minutes apart and the increased feeling of pressure. I gave the phone back to Franco when another wave of pain swept over me. When it passed enough for me to think clearly again, I looked to Franco for an answer. He'd opened a first aid box and had taken out a pair of surgical gloves.

"Rashid, go into the bathroom and bring back all the clean towels you can find," Franco commanded. As soon as Rashid got up, Franco took his place.

"Tess, the midwife said you might be ready to push. We need to get those panties off so I can gauge where you're at, okay?"

"No, Franco, I can't let you see my, aargh—" The contraction lasted so much longer this time, and the pressure down there was more intense. I wasn't sure whether I needed the toilet. I remembered them talking about that in an antenatal class. Some women said they felt like they would shit themselves when they were pushing. I was horrified at the time, and even more so now. Not only were these men about to find out what my vagina looked like, but they were probably going to see me shit myself.

"I feel like I'm going to shit myself, Franco," I told him as he was easing my knickers down my legs. Then I burst into tears until another contraction had me groaning that I couldn't do this anymore.

"It's normal to feel like that when you're ready to push, Tess. It says so in the books," Ivan said reassuringly.

I tilted my head to the side and glared at him. "Normal? How is any of this fucking normal, Ivan? And I'm certain that letting his boss's wife shit in his hands wasn't in Franco's job description."

Ivan was smart enough not to tell me off about my swearing this time. He preferred his balls attached to his body.

Rashid came from the bathroom with a smile on his face. He laid a couple of towels on the bed and said, "The boss is on his way. Jonesy said they've just left Whitehall. Call him, Tess. He's desperate to speak to you." Ivan handed me my phone just as Kolya video called me.

"I'm on my way, Tess. I'm sorry it's taken so long. I should have been there with you."

Franco slid a towel underneath me and told me to pull my knees up and open my legs. My bathrobe fell open to just under my bust, but I didn't attempt to close it. He put on the blue surgical gloves, saying, "The midwife said I have to feel how dilated you are. She said you shouldn't push until you're ten centimetres, which is about this much." He showed me with his fingers and thumb how wide that was, then waited until another contraction had passed until he examined me. It wasn't just uncomfortable, it was painful, too, and Franco couldn't apologise enough for hurting me.

Kolya had been reassuring me that everything was going to be all right, but Ivan's voice rose above his.

"How far gone is she, Franco?"

"She's ready now. So, Tess, on your next contraction, you can start to push, okay?"

I nodded at Franco, then looked down at my phone screen.

"Kolya, I can't do this without you. How long will you be?"

"About ten minutes, that's all. I love you, Tess, and I know you can do this. It wasn't what I wanted for you, but I know you are strong enough to deliver our baby anywhere. You are amazing, my darling."

I watched my rounded belly tighten when the next contraction hit, but I didn't attempt to push, even though Franco and Ivan encouraged me to.

"I'm sorry," I wailed. "I panicked. I think you're all wrong. I can't do it. I want Nan."

"What are you doing?" I heard Ivan ask.

"I'm getting YouTube up on my phone for Tess," Rashid replied. He stood behind us, leaning against the wall.

"She's about to have a baby, Rashid, she's not fucking bored!" Ivan stated before placing his hands on my belly and apologising to the baby for swearing.

"I know that, you bloody fool. I was bringing up videos on this stage of labour. When Julie had the girls, they told her she had to stop pushing for a bit. She had to pant instead," he replied.

"Was it when the head came out?" Ivan asked.

"I don't know. I wasn't at the business end," Rashid told him. His phone beeped with an incoming message.

"The staff have just delivered more clean towels and bedding. I'll bring them in, then I'll go back and check on security."

Franco watched him leave and then turned to look at me.

"When this next contraction comes along, I want you to push with everything you got, okay? Ivan's holding you nice and steady, and I'm gonna place your foot on my chest so you can bear down and push against me. You ready, Tess?"

Franco's handsome face had lost the pinched, worried look from earlier. His classic Italian features were set and determined. His dark brown eyes focused on nothing but my hot, sweaty face. I nodded and grimaced as another wave of pain hit me hard.

"Now, Tess. Remember what they said in class. Do it as if you are pushing through your bottom," Ivan encouraged. I pushed as hard as I could, but my efforts barely lasted ten seconds before I was gasping for breath in utter agony.

"I can't! It's just not working. I'm not strong enough, Ivan, and it's too hot in here."

"You *can* do it, baby," Franco insisted. "You're one of the strongest women I know. You've got a whole lotta strength, bravery, and resilience running through your veins and that baby in there can't wait to meet its mommy. So we're gonna remove your robe and drape a sheet over you so you can cool down a little, then we can start again on your next contraction, okay?"

"But I'm not wearing a bra," I panted. "You're all going to see my boobs."

"Tess, I'm about to watch your vagina stretch to the size of your baby's head, so trust me, you having your tits on show ain't gonna bother me one iota," Franco stated.

I groaned in embarrassment as Ivan opened my bathrobe and tugged it off my shoulders. He draped a sheet over my upper body and tucked it under my arms.

Ivan brought his arms down to my sides and slipped his fingers through mine. I tilted my head back to look at him, and he smiled down at me.

"Just think, Tess. We'll be able to hold your baby soon. I can't wait to tell him or her how much their uncle Ivan loves them."

"Trust me, Ivan, they already know. You've been telling them through my belly for months."

"I don't want the baby to be afraid of me, Tess. I'm so very tall, and that frightens some children." He looked so serious and forlorn. So unlike Ivan.

"How could anyone be frightened of you, Ivan? You're like a big, handsome, blue-eyed teddy bear. All this baby will want to do is cuddle you, so I hope you're ready for the babysitting duties you're going to get." He smiled down at me, then kissed the top of my head.

I gripped his hands tightly and pushed with all I had on the next two contractions, and for some reason, the pain didn't seem as bad, or I was just coping better than I had before. Ivan massaged my shoulders in between each contraction and gave me sips of water. He also wet the edge of a towel and wiped my forehead and the back of my neck.

The heaviness and pressure down below increased. This was really going to happen, whether I had medical assistance or not.

Kolya entered the bedroom, and I burst into tears with utter relief.

"I thought you wouldn't get here on time," I admitted.

"I'm so sorry, Tess. They had to be sure that explosives hadn't been left near the cars. The ambulance is on its way, and they're sending a doctor as well as a midwife."

"Why do we need a doctor? It's because it's happening too quickly, isn't it? Something's going to go wrong."

"Of course not, darling. But I'm paying them a small fortune, so I insisted that we also had a doctor present," he murmured while kissing me all over my face.

"You mean you threatened them or offered to pay them a ridiculous amount," I replied breathlessly as another contraction hit my tired body. Kolya encouraged me to push and placed my other foot against his chest. The pain seemed to go on and on, and the burning feeling down below was sheer agony. I had barely thirty seconds between the last contraction and the next.

"I can't do it," I cried.

"But you are doing it, Tess. I can see the baby's head." Kolya sounded so excited. He was staring between my legs with a look of complete awe.

"Just one more push, and then I want you to pant, okay, Tess?" Franco didn't wait for my reply. He was taking directions from someone—the midwife, I realised. I wondered how long he'd had her on speakerphone.

I hit a point where I kind of floated above the awful burning/stinging pain. Yes, it hurt, but it was as if I could leave the hurt for a few seconds in between pushes.

When Franco told me to stop pushing and start panting, the order didn't compute with me. I did nothing but stare at him. Both Kolya and Ivan kept repeating the word *pant* while panting in unison. Their continued verbal and visual directive finally kicked in, and I panted through the searing pain, watching Kolya's face change the more he glanced down.

"Just one more big push, Tess, and you can say hello to your baby." Franco sounded both excited and relieved.

It took more than one push, but the instant relief I felt when I finally delivered my baby was immense.

"We have a daughter, Tess. She's beautiful!" Kolya exclaimed.

"Let me see her," I demanded. I looked down to find Kolya wrapping a towel around her before placing her in my arms.

My daughter gazed up at me with her father's ice-blue eyes. Her lips were pursed, her fingers outstretched. Kolya kissed me softly on the lips before kissing our little girl on her forehead.

"She's amazing, Kolya. Look how long her fingers are," I remarked. Kolya touched his finger against her palm, and she gripped it tightly. The rush of elation on seeing my daughter for the first time overrode the exhaustion I'd felt only seconds before.

"She's so strong already. You did well, my darling. Thank you for giving me the chance to be a father again. I cannot express how much this means to me."

Kolya's eyes were full of happy tears, but it was Ivan who broke first.

Still sitting behind me, he took both Kolya and me in his arms and hugged us as he sobbed, mumbling sweet words of love for our little girl in English and Russian.

"Thank you, Franco," Kolya said, his voice choked with tears.

"Yes, thank you, Franco. I couldn't have done this without you. Come and have a good look at her. She's so pretty," I told him.

"I know. She's just like her mommy. But she's got her daddy's eyes, that's for sure." He kissed my cheek and added, "Hospital next time, Tess. I'm not cut out for this."

"Really? I was thinking of naming you Dr Franconni," I joked.

Chapter Thirty-One

KOLYA

The doctor stayed with Tess for less than thirty minutes, but the midwife was with her for at least three hours. My wife and daughter were perfectly healthy and didn't need to go to the hospital, although Tess was extremely tired.

I took her into the bathroom and helped her get clean and into her pyjamas. I was happy to help. Not being here when she needed me was torture.

Luckily, no one was killed in the terrorist attacks, although several people were seriously injured. The police had arrested eight men and one woman, but they hadn't revealed their identities.

I would like to get my hands on those nine people and introduce them to the effects of my latest cache of weaponry. Each bullet I fired at them would represent every minute they kept me away from my beautiful wife in her hour of need.

Nan had been stuck in the theatre with her sister until the police deemed it safe. The trains were running erratically due to the extra security checks, so Lucas was picking them up and taking her sister home before returning here with Nan. She was desperate to see our little cherub and insisted I send enough photos for her to fawn over until she could cuddle her.

With one hand, I adjusted the chair in my office before connecting to my family in Russia. I would have preferred to do this with James first, but he was flying back to the UK right now, having boarded our plane with his guards thirty minutes before Tess had given birth. Due to adverse weather over the Atlantic, James and I could not maintain a secure connection via video link. However, I'd spoken to him as soon as I was able and sent him at least a dozen photographs. I couldn't wait for him to meet his sister. To have them together in the same room would mean everything to me.

"Kolya." My father's voice came through before the image of him and Yuri appeared on the screen.

Speaking in Russian, I told them that Tess had an eventful day and was sleeping, but I had someone I wanted to introduce them to.

"Say hello to Lily Ivana Barinov," I told them as I carefully held my daughter in full view of the camera.

"A girl!" my father stated. I was prepared for him to be disappointed, so his following words surprised me. "I've always wanted a granddaughter to spoil. Look how beautiful she is, Yuri. She has our eyes, but I see her mother's pretty features."

I removed her white cotton cap and revealed a light covering of copper-coloured hair. My father and Yuri burst out laughing.

"She will also have her mother's fiery temper, brother," Yuri said as he wiped his eyes. "The hair does not lie. If you ever have to deny her anything, do it from the protection of an armoured vehicle."

"Tess might have a quick temper, but she certainly isn't demanding and was never spoilt by anyone as a child," I told them.

"But Lily is my granddaughter—the first little princess in our family. How can I deny her anything, Kolya? She is the most beautiful baby I have ever seen. You must bring her to Moscow as soon as she can travel. I cannot wait to hold her."

Roman Barinov was enamoured, but then again, so was everyone who'd seen my precious baby girl.

"How is my daughter-in-law? I would have liked to speak with her."

I proceeded to tell my father and Yuri everything that had happened today. When I ended the conversation, they were more impressed than ever with my strong, resilient wife. They already adored her, but now she'd given my family another child to love. There was no greater gift than that in my father's eyes.

Lily turned her head and began rooting against my shirt, expressing her hunger. The midwife had helped Tess get our little one latched on and suckling, but she hadn't been at her mother's breast long before falling asleep.

———

When I entered our bedroom, Tess was just beginning to stir.

"Lily's getting hungry again. She's been so busy charming our staff and my father and brother, it's no wonder she needs sustenance."

Tess got herself comfortable and unbuttoned her

pyjama top. She removed the breast pad, then exposed her left breast and held out her arms. It took her a couple of tries before Lily latched on.

Catherine hadn't breastfed James, so I found the entire process a fascinating and moving experience.

"How's Ivan now?" Tess asked as I adjusted the pillows so I could sit on the bed beside her.

"Drunk, and Franco is well on his way. Jonesy said he'll make sure they don't have any more." Ivan had hit the vodka hard in celebration of my daughter's birth.

"I can't believe how much he cried. First when she was born and then when he found out her middle name was Ivana. He's going to spoil her rotten, Kolya."

"I doubt he'll be the only one doing that. Everyone I've spoken to is smitten with her already. James dropped everything to fly over here as soon as I told him you were in labour, and Yannis and Jean are arriving in the morning. It took me a while to get Jonesy and Nate to hand Lily back when they'd held her."

"It's good to know she'll have so many people to love and care for her, Kolya. All children should have that."

"They should, my love. You should have had that, too. But what you lacked then, you have in droves now."

"I do," she replied, gazing down at our daughter. "I have a family to love and care for, and it's all thanks to you."

"If you hadn't saved my life, I wouldn't even be here, Tess. And we wouldn't have Lily, either. If thanks are given, they should go to you."

I turned her face to mine and kissed her softly. Tess tasted of sweet familiarity. She tasted like she was mine. My future, my always.

There was nothing I would not do for this woman and the child feeding at her breast. And my son, who is flying home to be with us. They are the reason my heart is over-flowing with love, pride, and joy.

My beloved family, my entire world.

They make me want to be a better man, but that's not an easy task when you are the son of a Bratva king.

Since meeting Tess, I have become more like a pakhan, and though it disturbs me, I do not regret killing the men who threatened my wife.

If anyone tries to harm my family, they will die at my hands. That is something that will never change. Protecting them should not be a crime, no matter how it's done.

Family is everything. Always.

Next in The Runaway Series

vinci-books.com/therunawaysruin

Love, loyalty, and lies—how much can one heart take?

Tess has embraced motherhood and life as an arms dealer's wife, despite the constant security. But when a lurking threat strikes, her world shatters. In the chaos, she learns love and loyalty aren't always what they seem. Can she rebuild her life—or is it too late?

Turn the page for a free preview…

The Runaway's Ruin: Chapter One

KOLYA

I'd had my warning. We all had. When we arrived home, we were to act suitably scared. Of course, I knew what I was about to see. My wife couldn't wait to send me photographs of my darling daughter all dressed up for Halloween. I have to say; she was the cutest little witch I'd ever seen. And it's not because I have a father's bias. Each of my guards agreed she was indeed the most beautiful little witch that ever wore a pointy hat.

Lily Ivana Barinov is a four-year-old replica of her mother, with the same copper-coloured curls, although she has my ice-blue eyes. She's a smart and tenacious little whirlwind who captures your attention with little effort. Oh, yes. It is safe to say my daughter is the star of our show. And I don't just mean for her mother and me. Lily is adored by everyone around her.

Ivan was smitten from the moment he knew Tess was pregnant. He's always had a lot of time and patience with children, but Lily is his world. They have a bond that even *I* am envious of.

I know that Yannis, too, is jealous of their bond. My friend is *all about* my daughter. The man is obsessed. He flew a designer in to decorate Lily's room in his villa to match her favourite book character, *Anna, The Little Princess*. He even had my tech guys install the same security system they designed for me to keep *his* little princess safe. I have seen more of Yannis in the four years since Lily was born than in all the years I've known him. Yannis says Lily brings joy to his life, along with a sense of peace within his heart, as if she could make everything right in his world.

Yannis had been close to my son. More like an uncle than a family friend. But James is now a very busy man: a twenty-five-year-old who barely has time to come home and see us from his base in America, never mind anyone else. He video calls Lily twice a week, and of course, I see him whenever we conference call for work purposes. Tess, Lily, and I fly over to stay with him two or three times a year, so it doesn't seem so bad for us.

Children become adults, and their need for you diminishes with the passing of time. I couldn't be prouder of the man my son has become, and KOLCAT US is thriving in his capable hands.

My father and elder brother, Yuri, dote on both Lily and James in a way I thought I would never see. Especially from my father. He calls Lily his *zolotse*, proclaiming she's precious to him. His greatest treasure.

Since we lost my brother, Aleksei, and his wife, Talia, in a light aircraft accident over the coast of Monaco, my father hasn't been the same man he once was. None of us has.

I will never forget the day I received the call that they were missing. The coastguard and another rescue team were combing the area below their last reported location for days. Ivan had met with Aleksei whilst on holiday just hours before, so he was first on the scene. My father and I sent in our own teams, yet in the end, it was just a recovery mission. Although in our hearts, we'd known that from the start. We found some of the wreckage from their plane along with their luggage, but the sea had claimed their bodies, adding even more to our distress.

That was almost seventeen months ago, although it often seems like yesterday. As much as I distanced myself from my father in my younger years, since Aleksei's death, I've felt the need to be near both him and Yuri—despite them being so entrenched in the ugliness that is Bratva.

To that end, I have been pursuing a goal I once had with regard to operating a KOLCAT build site with the backing of the European Council for Business. Last month, I finally received the news that they fully supported my plans, so I purchased a large parcel of land I'd had my eye on in Estonia. With Ivan flying me to the airport, I can be in Moscow with my father within two hours. I'm hoping to convince Tess we need a holiday home there, though that won't be easy.

Sarah's Legacy, the charity we set up over four years ago, has gone from strength to strength. For a time, Tess, Jean, and Karen Foster—a former police officer who'd been involved in the investigation into Sarah's murder—were at the helm. However, due to the charity's success, we had to recruit two more regional managers after branching out into another two cities. Tess and Karen had been studying together on various courses to aid their managerial roles, so they hadn't spent enough time with Jean to notice those first subtle changes.

A member of staff in the Sheffield branch became concerned and alerted Tess to Jean's progressive forgetfulness and other strange behaviour. When we went to see her, she seemed fine.

Jean told us she'd been feeling a little under the weather due to lack of sleep. I wasn't so sure that was the only thing bothering her.

Sharon, the woman who'd been in contact with us, said she was concerned that Jean was acting the same as her aunt when she was in the early stages of dementia. So I left Lucas with Jean in the guise of him helping with deliveries and moving furniture around the office. After three days, he confirmed that Jean was certainly not herself. He said that minutes after she'd begun a task, she'd become confused and unsure of what she should be doing, although it wasn't happening all the time. Sometimes, she was just the same Jean we all knew and loved so dearly.

Tess and I went with her to see her doctor, and when he advised her to see a specialist, I was happy to pay to ensure that happened quickly. After numerous tests, they confirmed what we all feared: Jean had dementia.

Despite medication and help with retaining cognitive function, Jean's dementia was still progressing more rapidly than we expected. Understandably, Tess was devastated to hear this, and so was I. I felt as lost and as helpless regarding Jean's condition as I did with my mother's and aunt's cancer.

If there *is* a god up there in the heavens, he can fuck off as far as I'm concerned. He messes with and takes away the lives of good people. People who believe in him. My brother's wife was a believer; it hadn't saved her when their plane went down.

If God wants to target people, he should take aim at men like Mohammed Riass, the lying fucker who claimed to be a Turkish government minister of the same name. From what my sources tell me, along with other reliable information I have gathered, Riass is a prominent leader of a new breakaway ISIS terrorist group, who've been targeting Kurdish freedom fighters with some success. They've also been involved in terrorist activity along the Serbian border of Albania, and more worryingly for me and my team, Riass had links to a terrorist cell in the UK, which was discovered last year during several counter-terrorism raids. A friend who works for MI5 told me they'd found information on me and my family—photos and regular routines— as well as the main UK KOLCAT build site.

Riass was interested in a new weapon we sold to a Saudi buyer. The missile launcher has the usual long-range capabilities of our previous models. It's an exceptional weapon with changeable ground clearance and two target-width options, making it more adaptable for air and ground-based offensive manoeuvres. B26319-7 is hardly revolutionary in terms of what it can do, but it's easily transportable over most terrain due to its lean build and its trailer's adaptability. It can also be programmed both on the launcher and remotely. Again, that's not unique to this kind of weapon. What is somewhat unique is that the missiles fired can be detonated remotely with targeted precision at any point, which is rarely seen in anything other than nuclear weaponry. I designed the weapon myself, so my team and I will fly over to stay with the buyer, Prince Amir— the Deputy Defence Minister of Saudi Arabia—to give further demonstrations and all the relevant programmable codes. Codes that only one other technician and I have knowledge of.

The new weapon and the plans for the operations base in Estonia have kept me away from my family more than my wife and I are happy with.

Tess wants another child, which I'm more than thrilled about. When I was home last week, we talked about her stopping the Depo injection, but as she'd rightly pointed out, despite not taking contraceptive measures, we'd still need to have sex to make a baby, something we can't do if I'm away with KOLCAT.

I've promised my wife I'll cut my stay with the prince as short as possible, and then I'll take a full month off work. Of course, I'm off to Estonia first. Yet another trip away from my beloved.

I'm lucky to have her; I know this with everything I am. My beautiful Tess has just turned twenty-three. I'm almost twice her age, and it shows.

I shaved off my beard last year and keep my hair short now. I was sick of seeing all the grey creeping in and taking over my face and the sides of my head. It's still there, of course, but I'm not as conscious of it as I was. Tess says it doesn't bother her that I'm older; she remarked that she actually fancies me with grey hair. Be that as it may, I don't feel comfortable with it.

It doesn't help when I know there are younger men who want her. She turns heads wherever she goes, though she still doesn't see her appeal.

I suppose, in a way, we are one and the same, she and I. We both have our insecurities, though I never felt this way before Tess. I feel less confident. Vulnerable. Neither of those feelings sit well with me.

There's a young man working in the Manchester office of Sarah's Legacy who fawns over Tess and looks at her like she hung the moon. It's clear to see he wants her. I'd have said something about it if not for how much it pisses Franco off whenever he's near.

Oh, yes, I know *all* about Franco. I've known he's been

in love with her for the longest time. I knew when he offered to marry Tess to prevent her from going back into care. Some people would think I was crazy to employ a man who's in love with my wife, but to me, it serves a purpose. He's her bodyguard; it's his job to protect her. It's the same with all my guards. But due to how strongly Franco feels about Tess, his senses will be sharper, and his need to protect her much keener. When you love someone so deeply, you don't need to see or hear the danger coming their way; you have a knowing you feel in your very soul. There's no training available to give a bodyguard that same kind of edge. I keep him around because he'll keep Tess safe or die trying. If that makes me cruel, then so be it.

Too bad he's a good-looking bastard.

I trust my wife completely. She's a regular eye-roller when it comes to men flirting with her. It used to make her uncomfortable, but that's changed over the years. It's clear to see she has no interest in anyone else. She looks at me with such love and adoration and, lately, a little sadness, which is why, next month, I will make it up to her. We will take the yacht I bought her for her twenty-first birthday and sail around the Bahamas. We can spend our days together as a family, enjoying precious time with our daughter. But when the sun goes down, Tess will be all mine. I'll fill our nights with passionate encounters, the likes of which we will never forget.

The Runaway's Ruin: Chapter Two

KOLYA

Two members of my new security team were at the gates of my home in Oxford as we approached. After speaking to Jonesy, they opened them and let us through. One of those guards at the gates today came from Yannis's security team.

Darius Anagnos had wanted to move to England for years. His aunt and uncle owned a cafe in Wimbledon, and he wanted to be nearer to them. His parents had passed away, and his aunt and uncle were the only family he had left. After three years of asking if I would take him, I finally gave in to Yannis's demands. I hired Darius around four months ago, though I still had my team bring him up to scratch. Although he'd served three years in the Greek military, he was nowhere near the level of my security detail.

Ivan and Franco don't get along with him. In fact, I'd go as far as saying Ivan detests him, though most of the other guards and I find Darius to be an unassuming man who follows orders well.

I added five new members to our close protection team when Lily was born, one of those being a female ex-army medic from the US. Her name is Lainey Palmer, and she's as tough as she is beautiful. All my team adore her, and although she's the only female member, she gets along well with every one of my guards.

I brought Lainey in as my daughter's personal guard, and as far as Tess was concerned, I couldn't have picked anyone better. Being both a trained soldier *and* a medic ticked the right boxes, and the fact that she's a natural with children was the icing on the cake.

Mark Rush and Greg Cassidy are another two close protection guards I brought on board. Both are ex-Marines who fit in seamlessly; it's almost as if they've been part of my team since day one. Mark's also an accomplished helicopter pilot, which has come in handy whenever Ivan's been away.

As we made our way up the long driveway, I keyed in Lily's date of birth on my phone, switching on the live camera feed to my home to find out where my darling wife and daughter were. I couldn't locate them anywhere in the extension—where we lived—so I transferred the feed to the old manor house where my guards resided. I found them making their way along the second floor, knocking on the doors of each of our guards' rooms. It was as close as Lily would get to the regular trick-or-treating other children do at Halloween. It's just not safe for a child of mine to do anything so public.

Tess insists Lily has as normal an upbringing as possible, although we had to make several compromises. She'd attended a local playgroup three half-days per week from her being two years old. Initially, the group seemed wary about the guards who had to accompany her. But after I gave them a sizeable monetary donation, which enabled them to purchase new books, toys, and other much-needed items, they readily accepted Lily's protective entourage. The women were particularly fond of Ivan, and I'm told he'd been propositioned by more than one of them. Being a six-foot-eight wall of muscle, his height and build usually intimidated people, but it seemed the mothers and nannies attending Happy Tots Playgroup in Oxford were up to the challenge of taming my Russian behemoth cousin.

Tess said they loved Ivan because he took an interest in the women *and* their children, remembering their names and asking how their weekend went. They liked that he paid attention. Of course, he did have an ulterior motive when doing so.

Each parent/caregiver of Happy Tots was investigated thoroughly by my team, as well as the parents and teachers at the infant school she is now attending. Lainey is allowed to stay in the classroom with Lily in the guise of a classroom assistant/helper. Ivan, too, if he's not guarding Tess.

Andy, another new guard, stays outside the classroom, with Dave guarding the school gates. It's a lot of organisation, but seeing my daughter's smiling face and the constant chatter about her school day makes it worthwhile. I would do anything to make my wife and daughter happy. Anything at all.

Once the car stopped outside my home, my guards and I got out as quietly as possible and made our way to the kitchen, filling our pockets with various sweets and chocolate bars from a bowl Nan had filled in readiness. She had a huge smile, telling me how excited my daughter had been all day. They'd trimmed up most of the house with various *scary* Halloween decorations, and Lily had been wearing her witch outfit since breakfast.

Last month, my father had sent Lily a gift after she'd complained that there were no dolls with the same curly red hair as she had. The doll was the spitting image of Lily, with copper-coloured curls the same size as both her and her mother's and uncannily realistic eyes. I thought it a little creepy if I'm honest, and as it was the same height as my daughter, it wasn't so easy to avoid looking at it. Lily calls the doll Anna, after the princess in her favourite stories. She insists on dressing Anna in her princess gown, which still sheds glitter months after she received it, although, from the photographs in the messages I'd just opened, Anna was also dressed as a witch for Halloween.

My phone buzzed again, this time with a message from Kevin telling me that Lily and Tess were approaching, so everyone went quiet to listen for a knock at the door.

"Trick or treat, a penny or a sweet!" my little darling proclaimed with an excited giggle before knocking loudly.

We all gathered at the door, and right on cue, everyone feigned being shocked and scared as I opened it.

Lily laughed out loud before leaping into my open arms. "It's only me, Daddy. I'm not really a witch. Look—I'm just Lily!"

She took off her black pointy hat and held up her basket full of treats.

"Trick or treat, everybody?"

After giving her the treats I'd pocketed, I gave her a quick kiss, then let her go so my guards could spoil her. Tess stepped into my line of vision, grinning widely.

"Trick or treat, Kolya?"

I tugged my beautiful wife against me, whispering "Treat" before kissing her soft, candy-flavoured lips.

"Later," she replied. "I promise a night full of Halloween treats after the party."

Her amber eyes shone with mirth and a wicked glint that excited my travel-weary body. She pulled away from me and walked towards Lily. Her basket was overflowing with the sweeties she'd been given, so Tess began the task of convincing her to save some of her haul for another day.

Glancing back at the doorway, I found Yannis filming everything on his phone.

"I thought I would capture a few special moments from today so you can look at them when you aren't busy working," he said somewhat testily.

Why did he always feel the need to have a dig at me? He knew my meeting was important. If it weren't, I wouldn't have taken it.

Yannis had been pissing me off lately with his sarcastic remarks and endless visits. Nearly every time I came back home, he was here, giving me grief for being away from my family. Tess didn't like him turning up out of the blue, either. He was supposed to meet us in London so we could all go to the party together, yet here he was again, invading my home life. I would have enjoyed spending time with my wife and daughter before we left.

No wonder his business was doing so poorly. He was never there to do anything about it.

Yannis hadn't told me about the company's problems; I found out from his cousin, who is one of the shareholders. For the past six years, the shipbuilding and hotel empire his father and grandfather created had been losing money fast. It was probably the reason he was so angry with me when I didn't buy one of his shipyards. Although, I did purchase his yacht for Tess's twenty-first birthday a little over two years ago. I paid him ninety-five million euros, an amount that Tess couldn't get her head around. It was already five years old when I bought it, but I knew it was an absolute steal for the spec on that vessel. The yacht was named Princess Annis, but neither Tess nor I referred to it by anything other than *the yacht*. I asked her if she wanted to change the name, but she didn't feel the need.

We'd already sailed to the Cayman Islands, as well as the Bahamas, which Tess adored. She also preferred to stay on the yacht than with Yannis whenever we visited his island, although we did spend the occasional night in his home to appease him.

Like me, Tess values our private time as a family, which Yannis should appreciate. After all, as he so often makes a point of telling me, I should not be missing out on all the precious moments with my wife and daughter.

Before I could give Yannis a clever comeback, Ivan walked into the kitchen from the tech room and told us we'd been granted a 5 p.m. flight time, which gave me just over an hour to spend with my daughter.

The Runaway's Ruin: Chapter Three

TESS

Nan was busy in the kitchen serving us hot roast pork sandwiches, although Lily and Danny had cheese. Bess hung around the table, begging for scraps again. I swear that dog should have been twice the size for the amount she ate. It didn't help that everyone kept feeding her. She was a master at the "*I'm so hungry because nobody ever feeds me*" eyes. I once saw Ivan cook a twenty-two-ounce sirloin steak just for her.

Lily sat on Kolya's knee, telling him about the new game Lainey and I had been teaching her.

"You have to have lots of squares with numbers in them. It's called scopscotch," she said before taking a bite out of her sandwich. She kept trying to speak with her mouth full until Kolya told her to wait until she'd swallowed all of it. She opened her mouth to show him the bite was all gone before telling him how to play.

"Sometimes there's one square, and sometimes it's two, but you're only allowed to put one foot in each square. And you have to hop—that's when you jump on one foot. Oh, and you have to throw a stone into the square, and then you hop to it and pick it up when you come back," she informed him.

"I remember playing that on the street when I was a little girl," Nan told her. "It's called hopscotch."

"That's what I said, Nan. Scopscotch," Lily replied.

Kolya stifled a laugh before asking, "Do you like the game, Lily?"

She took a moment to consider his question.

"Well, I'm not very good at hopping and balancing. Not like Mummy and Lainey. But I'm better than Ivan because his feet are too big for the squares, and Mummy says if your feet go over the lines of the square, it's cheating."

Kolya looked at Ivan and burst out laughing.

"I wasn't cheating," Ivan protested. He pointed at Lainey and declared, "It's her fault for making the squares too small."

"If I'd made them any bigger, Lily would've needed to do more than one hop to get to the next square," Lainey replied.

"Please tell me someone filmed Ivan attempting to play hopscotch?" Kolya begged, still laughing at the thought of his cousin hopping around.

Franco held up his phone. "I did, boss. Sorry it's jumpy. It's difficult to film when you're laughing so hard."

Everyone around the table scrambled for Franco's phone while the man this was all about grabbed another sandwich.

The thing about Ivan is he couldn't care less what anyone thinks about him. He'll do anything Lily asks without a single complaint. Lily's happiness is more important to him than anyone thinking he looks foolish or unmanly. And, let's face it, I doubt Ivan could ever look unmanly. With his height, frame, and the plethora of tattoos he's accumulated, Ivan has that stereotypical image of being mean and dangerous, something I know he plays upon when the situation requires it. But Ivan has a softness that he reserves for those he loves. His stunning blue eyes light up whenever Lily's around, and when he smiles, he melts your heart. Of course, I've also seen Ivan's flirty side. When he gives the ladies his *sexy-eyed come-on*, then follows it with that half smile and raised brow... No wonder all the women at playgroup used to fawn all over him. One woman even had the cheek to ask me if I'd ever seen him naked, and if so, was he as big all over as she'd been imagining?

Lily slid down from her father's knee and walked around the table to Ivan. When he lifted her into his arms, she hugged him tightly, saying, "We'll chalk you some bigger squares next time, Ivan. I'll just do more hops."

Ivan smiled, then kissed her forehead. "Thank you, my little Lilypot. You know I love you very much, don't you?"

"I love you more, Ivan," she replied.

My heart always seems to do a little flip whenever Lily and Ivan have one of their adoringly sweet moments. Knowing that someone loves her as much as Kolya and I do is so reassuring. I know if ever anything happens to her father and me, she'll be well taken care of. Lily will never have the same childhood experiences I had. She'll never know what it's like to go without food, warmth, and love.

Of course, there's not only Ivan who adores our little girl. Nan, Jack, Yannis, and each of our guards have a soft spot for her, especially Lainey, Danny, Jonesy, Nate, Kevin, and Franco—the man who helped me deliver her safely into the world. Since that most special time, I've become so much closer to Ivan and Franco. We shared an experience none of us will ever forget. They were my strength that day in so many ways. I love them both dearly and can't imagine my life without them in it.

While everyone else was trying to get a look at the video of Ivan hopscotching, Yannis and Darius—our guard who used to work for him—began speaking to each other in Greek, their voices low. I wasn't having that. It's just plain rude. And to be honest, Yannis had pissed me off all day with his snide comments in front of Lily about Kolya rarely being around, so that was the last straw for me.

"Yannis, Darius, I'll have none of that here. You know the rules. If you want to go off somewhere and speak in your own language, that's fine, but while you're in our company, it's not acceptable. It's almost like you're whispering behind your hands about us. I don't allow it from Kolya and Ivan, so I won't have it from you two, either."

I'd made that rule within the first six months of living here. If Kolya and Ivan switch to Russian, it usually means they're arguing. If they have a blazing row in English, at least I can intervene and calm them down.

Darius apologised quickly, though he looked less than sorry. Yannis smirked at me before saying, "I'm sorry, Mother."

I pushed my chair back from the table and stood as tall as possible.

"I wasn't joking, Yannis. This is my house, and those are my rules. If you don't like it, you know where the door is, which also applies to Darius. Both of you speak good English, so there's no need to revert to Greek while you are in our company. Doing so shows a level of disrespect I find particularly repugnant."

Since having Lily, I've tried to cut back on my swearing, at least in her presence. It helps when dealing with the business side of the charity, too. Karen Foster taught me to take a deep breath and find a word or phrase that's more socially acceptable when dealing with people you'd rather tell to fuck off. Jonesy says I sound like I've swallowed a dictionary, but my husband definitely approves.

Ivan handed Lily back to Kolya and came to stand behind me, resting his hands on my shoulders while Franco moved to my left. The room became unnervingly quiet, apart from the odd rustling of sweet wrappers from Lily, who seemed oblivious to all but her Halloween treats.

"Kolya, I think you should pass your wife some of Lily's chocolate. She appears to be in a mood," Yannis declared with an eye roll. Darius snickered like a schoolboy at his response.

Kolya's pale blue eyes fixed on Yannis and Darius; that icy glare stopped any further snide remarks from his long-time friend.

"I suggest you think carefully before you open your mouth to speak again, Yannis. Aggravating my wife any further would not be a wise move on your part."

"Kolya, you know I didn't mean any harm." Yannis appeared surprised at Kolya's words. He held his hand over his heart. "Tess, my darling, you know me and my sense of humour. I swear I meant no offence."

"Then I suggest you think about some of the offhand comments you've been making today and consider the fact they lacked anything but sarcasm." I rolled the sleeves of my sweater up to my elbows and placed my hands on the table, holding his uncertain gaze.

"I might be a wife and mother now and live a life much different from the one I did as a young child and teenager, but I'm still no pushover. I don't need the man I married or the men at my back to fight my corner. So if you want to take me on, Yannis, go ahead. I guarantee you won't come out of it smiling."

I glanced over at Kolya, who was staring at me, his eyes hooded and filled with lust. Typical! Whenever he sees me get angry over something, it makes him want his wicked way with me. As much as I wanted that to happen, I knew we had to leave soon.

Yannis came around the table and stood before me with a genuine look of regret on his handsome face.

"Tess, please forgive me. I know I've upset you, and I am deeply sorry for doing so. Your friendship means the world to me, and I'd be lost without you in my life. Please… I'll do anything to make it up to you." He took my hands in his before kissing the back of them.

"Anything?" I asked innocently.

"Anything at all."

Grab your copy…
vinci-books.com/therunawaysruin

About the Author

Helen Bright was born and raised in Yorkshire, UK, and often bases her novels in and around the county.

Whether she's writing paranormal or contemporary romance, her novels often have darker elements hidden inside a deep and meaningful love story.

www.ingramcontent.com/pod-product-compliance
Lightning Source LLC
Chambersburg PA
CBHW011747010726
47498CB00012B/2965